Johnny

a great guy

June C. Mitchel

A Wedding In Georgia

by: June Weikel

A Wedding In Georgia
June E. Weikel

Editing: Susan Pelletier

Author's Photo: Michele Claeys

Cover Sketch: Ann Rothmyer

Cover Design and Typography: Anna McBrayer

Research: Lynn Weikel

ISBN # 1-887617-14-0

Published by
St. Barthelemy Press Ltd.
2971 Flowers Road South
Suite 100
Atlanta,GA 30341
(800)-451-1923

This book is dedicated with love and pride

To my brother

Kenneth Jones Weikel, Sr.

(Semper Fidelis)

A Wedding In Georgia

Chapter 1

It was almost noon on one of those hot, sticky July days we seemed to have so often in New Jersey. This may have been the summer of love for some— I heard all about those people up in Woodstock going wild—but for me, it was just plain old hot, so hot that the birds were pulling up worms with pot-holders. I wiped a trickle of sweat from the side of my face and scanned the sky for thunderclouds. No relief in sight. I finished cutting the front lawn and pushed the mower into the musky dark corner of the garage.

Weekends only allow me a short time to get all my chores done, and I had a lot of chores to do on that sticky Saturday. I put my clothes in the dryer, made myself a tomato sandwich, and sat down to my weekly store list. I made a separate list for the hardware store: two gallons of eggshell white paint, a couple of rollers and pans, some brushes, a buck-et, and some sponges. Having decided that I could not live with prison green kitchen, living room and dining room walls any longer; I was going to do some serious painting.

Maybe I could get the kitchen done today, I mused. Two walls, how long could it take? I also made a list for the cookout I was preparing that night. So the paint doesn't dry, who cares? I put a new toilet seat on the hardware list. A lavender seat with yellow walls would be great for Easter. It seems the couple I purchased this place from had bought any paint that was on sale. I'd better add a hammer and screwdriver. One of the men coming to my cookout could put the new toilet seat on for me.

The phone rang. It was Sam, short for Samantha. I meet many people in life: some are casual never see again types or those that you feel you want to spend time with again, some are a real pain in the ass. And then there are those rare people I meet who are like Sam. She has magic. She bubbles over with excitement, and you can't help but get caught up in it. She may irritate the hell out of me at times, but one thing you can say for Sam: Life's never boring when she's around.

Sam said, "Guess what, Megan?"

Now when Sam says, "Guess what?" I always have the feeling I should duck and cover.

You just never know what this female is planning. I figure it best not to say anything, just listen, so she continued.

"I have a great surprise. I am getting married in three weeks. We want you to come to the wedding and reception."

"I hear you, girl," I replied, feeling kind of shocked. I mean, Sam getting married? In three weeks? "Who are you marrying?" was all I could think of saying.

"Oh, silly I'm marrying Harry. We are having the wedding and reception in a small rural area outside of Macon."

"What are you telling me?" I said. "Are you telling me that you are marrying Harry the mechanic—that Harry? Have you gone completely out of your mind? Is this the same Sam who, with a few notable exceptions, dates only doctors, veterinarians, dentists, lawyers, and various others that have at least two professional designations after their names? You can't be serious."

"Serious as a heart attack," she said. "We were sitting in a bubble bath last night with a pitcher of sangria and Harry said, 'Let's get married.' I said, 'Why not?'"

"I know you, Sam; well enough that you like to rattle my cage. I also know that right now you are tugging on your left ear—you always do that when you're trying to either shock me or convince me you're telling the truth. You and Harry getting married?"

"Have you totally lost your frigging mind? Just tell me, are you that damn desperate?" I sighed, blew a stray piece of hair out of my face. "You have my blessings, girl," I said. "Consider the cookout here tonight your wedding supper gift from me."

"Oh silly, I don't think you are taking this news

well at all," she laughed. "But seriously, think about it. You are the one who's always telling me I should stop fooling around so much, that I should get serious with my life, serious with someone, instead of spending my life having a hell of a good time no strings attached. I thought you would be pleased." Her voice started to sound pouty, the way a little girl's does when she doesn't get what she wants.

"And instead, what do I get from you? Nothing but grief. What the hell do you want from me? Harry is very sexy. I mean, girlfriend, he is great. He knows what a girl wants. He is good under the hood and a hunk under the sheets."

I must have gasped or something, when she pounced. "That is still going on out there you know. Or maybe you don't. When was the last time you got laid? Just because you had a lousy marriage, now you can't be happy for me?"

Sam sighed, the anger seeping out of her voice. "You think I am crazy. Of course I am. You're right, but what you don't know it is hereditary, being raised in a frigging dysfunctional family. I don't believe my parents had sex either, I mean with each other, for years. Dear old Mother was too deep into her love affair with Jack Daniels, and my Daddy would never be picked father of the year." I could hear her shake her head, tossing off emotion like so much static electricity from a sweater. While she is one of the most emotional people I know, there are some places inside her that she just doesn't like to go. She'd rather be in her "Oh, silly mode". So I wasn't surprised when she dropped the subject abruptly, ending the conversation with a promise to stop at the bakery for a cheesecake for dessert that night.

Chapter 2

Needless to say, I didn't know what to make of the whole thing. Was she putting me on or what? With Sam it sometimes could be hard to tell, just the thought of Sam getting married? Somehow, I just couldn't see it. She loved having boyfriends, but a husband? I doubted it; I like Harry however, not as husband material for Sam.

Sam was in love with love and the chase. Just the idea that she could add a new name to her list of conquests was like her own private collection of her prize stud farm. I had to laugh just a little to myself, thinking about some of the collection she'd had. There   was this one particular great guy she had met when she was making arrangements after her poodle, Tyrone, passed on. She heard of this pet cemetery that had a chapel, viewing rooms, and a separate area where you could go to choose the type of casket or urn you'd like for your dearly departed. Well, Sam loved her Tyrone, and money was certainly no object. Let me tell you, that dog went out—or rather down—in style. The owner's son gave Sam the full-blown bereavement package; he even told her he would dig the grave himself. She could come to the cemetery two days before Tyrone was scheduled to be viewed, he said, pick out the spot she would like, and then he would prepare the opening in the ground where Tyrone would be inserted. Seems while he was digging this hole in the ground, Sam noticed how his body glistened with beads of sweat after he had removed his shirt. He had the smallest waist, she said, plus broad shoulders and a tight ass. He made her feel like she could have lain down on the mound of dirt and bare the throbbing pulsation she felt between her thighs right then and there. I later found out after we had couple glasses of wine, she did just that. She went out with this tight-ass hunk for about six months then, as usual, became bored and moved on.

She had just about used him up when she decided that Tyrone needed a tombstone. She located a place near the shore, and I went with her to pick one out. They had every picture you could think of in the catalog, but none suited her. I looked up from the catalog and saw her checking out this gorgeous curly-haired blond man with blue eyes. He had a good body—looked like he did a lot weight lifting—and also a way of standing in his tight jeans that Sam just couldn't resist. She gazed at him dreamily, hungrily, for a while, than came back to reality.

"What I would like is a stone shaped like a dog biscuit." She addressed the young hunk. "Can you do that?"

"No problem," he replied. "However, it will cost about ten or twenty dollars more. We have to make a sketch for your approval and you may have to make several trips until we are certain we get it right."

Sam smiled. "We'll get it right."

Driving back I knew Sam had something on her mind. "What do you think?" she asked.

"What do I think about what, Sam?"

"Do you think I did everything to make Tyrone happy? He was my baby, you know that. I was trying to think what else I could do for him."

"Now that you ask me, Sam, I was really surprised that you did not have Gladys Knight and the Pips sing 'Amazing Grace' when they lowered the casket into the ground."

The dog-biscuit-shaped marble was placed by the end of summer. The stone cutter was replaced shortly after that, though he no doubt gave one of his best grinding efforts to the stone and Miss Sam.

Shortly after that episode, Sam had some pains in her abdomen. I suggested that she see a doctor, and Sam made an appointment for an internal exam. She was a nervous wreck and insisted I go with her. She had said to me in a threatening tone that I had better go into the examining room with her. Those plans changed as soon as the doctor walked into the waiting room. He was a Rock Hudson look-a-like in a white lab jacket. Sam took one look and told me I could wait for her there.

When she came out, she was grinning like a schoolgirl, as we walked out of his office Sam stopped and turned to me "what hands, let me tell you girl friend this doctor is a vaginal engineer.

"And the pains?" I said.

"Oh that. Well, I have to take some medication as there is a possibility I have a slight infection. Nothing serious, thank goodness." Maybe her illness wasn't serious, but the doctor was. She soon was seeing him three nights a week, starting that night. And I don't mean professionally.

But the veterinarian had the longest track record of all.

Before Tyrone's demise, he was a frisky and happy poodle. Up until Sam took him for his annual rabies shot, that is. It seems the vet's son had replaced his aging father in the practice. All of a sudden, Tyrone seemed to need more check ups than a pregnant female about to give birth. Tyrone hated the vet and showed his vengeance when he came home by lifting his leg and peeing against Sam's expensive sofa. After two of these episodes, the vet began to make after-hours house calls. Sam was pleased; Tyrone hid under the bed until the vet left.

Then there was the dentist. He wanted to get serious, and for a while I thought maybe this would be the one. But like all the others, this affair petered out. It wasn't a total failure, though: she ended up with a great smile.

Smiling at the memories, I went about doing my chores. I made it to the hardware store, and stopped by the grocers to get the fixings for the cookout. As I unloaded the bags on the counter, sweat dripping down my nose, I decided to hell with the painting. Instead, I plopped myself on the couch and rested up for what looked like it might be a challenging evening ahead.

Surprisingly enough, Sam and Harry seemed to be their normal selves that night. The cookout was a great success. Sam sparkled and kept everyone laughing. It turned out just to be five of us: Sam, Harry, another couple, and me. George, an ambulance driver who was supposed to be my date, had called earlier to say they were very busy at the hospital and he could not get away. What else is new? I've never had Sam's luck with men, that's for sure. Sam and Harry left about ten, with not a word from Sam about our conversation that afternoon, and no mention of a wedding. Which I thought was curious, but I wasn't about to push it.

Sam made several comments about how much she liked the shorts and shirt I was wearing, and how they went well with my tan. It was unusual for her to pass a compliment, but I wasn't complaining. But Harry was the biggest surprise. He had cut his long hair, and instead of his usual grubbies he was wearing a pair of white slacks, a navy blue shirt, and sandals. Sam may or may not be marrying this guy, but she sure had taken him shopping. I must admit he was looking good. Sam was wearing this long sarong thing that was slit from her left thigh to the ankle, and high-heeled sandals. This did not resemble the cute little short set she told me about on the phone.

Chapter 3

Thinking I'd have a nightcap of scotch on rocks before bedding down, I shoved aside the painting supplies that littered my small kitchen and sat at the small table in the corner. Spotting the new toilet seat I forgot to ask Harry to replace, I figured that I'd start painting the kitchen tomorrow, and maybe just take on the toilet seat myself. How hard could it be? Anything would be better than sitting on an apple-green toilet seat in a burgundy and pink bathroom. Actually, when I bought the house, the entire bathroom was lavender. I didn't live with that for more than just a few weeks, but I just hadn't gotten around to replacing the commode seat.

I took a sip of the scotch, letting the smoky flavor linger on my tongue as I thought back to what Sam said to me on the phone about my lousy marriage. Was she really telling me that I had no right to criticize her if she chose to marry Harry? There's no doubt that I picked the wrong one to marry. We married for better or worse, but unfortunately, the better was brief and the worse ended up turning into the marriage from hell. But that was over years ago. Why did she have to bring that up, like I had to be reminded?

I took a bigger sip, and allowed myself to think back to those days. The first two years were good, I allowed, though that fact was hard to remember, given what came later. We had a small church service, and Anthony's brother stood for him. Sam was there for me, of course. I wore a light blue dress, and he wore a dark blue suit. We had the reception in the church fellowship hall where his mother had complete control of the choice of food and friends—they were all hers. My parents could not attend. My father had recently undergone serious surgery and could not travel. We had a low-budget honeymoon—two nights in Asbury Park—and moved into an efficiency apartment with just a kitchen, bedroom, and bath to save money toward buying a house.

Anthony, oh yes, Anthony. He was a tall, handsome, party-loving guy. That's where I met him, actually, at a friend's birthday party. He had a way about him, and it sure worked on me. Right from the start, I was in love. After dating for three months, he proposed. I was so love-struck; I could hardly even breathe the word "yes."

Sam was disgusted when I told her we were getting married. Over and over again during those three months we were dating, Sam kept telling me he was going to break my heart. She even went so far as to tell me she saw him with someone else when he was dating me. Which of course, I refused

Chapter 4

to believe.

I lived in blissful ignorance for those first two years, but then he started to lapse. He was coming home late, and I could tell that he had had a couple of drinks. Other times, he would come home, start an argument and then walk out, only to come home late. Then I started smelling perfume on his shirts, and it was not the kind of perfume I could have afforded. Of course, he would deny everything. He would call on the way home from work saying he was going to stop in to see his mother. And when he came home late, well, he said that she insisted he stay for dinner. Forget the fact that I had rushed home from my job to make him a special dinner. To hell with that, he would say, how could he hurt Mother?

One Friday he called me at work about noon, and said the boss wanted him to put in some extra hours. "Don't wait dinner," he said. Fine. Sam met me at the Seaboard Lounge for a drink after work about six. After we had a drink, we decided to have another, then a sandwich. She had no plans, and I certainly didn't, so we took our time. I told her Anthony called like he always did when he was working late. I said he told me to call Sam and go out for while. Sam said, "Yeah, sure, right. Guess who is coming through the door. And look, what a surprise, he's not alone."

Anthony was walking with a redhead toward the darkest corner of the lounge. He patted her ass as she was sitting down. He could not see us around the corner of the bar, but we could see him just fine. They ordered a drink and sat very close, like this was certainly not their first time together. She was wearing a white spaghetti strap dress that allowed the other on looking envious males to enjoy the fact that she was blessed with a matching pair of well developed breasts that were given all the freedom they wanted. Sam and I were certain that also applied to her lower treasure. She had the right moves such as leaning forward when she was listening to him talk and picking invisible lint from his tie or jacket. He never took his eyes away from her even when he was giving the waiter their dinner order.

We finished our drinks and left out the side door. We could have just as easily passed their table and left from the front entrance the way we came in, however I just made it clear that it was not the right time or place to make a scene.

Sam gave me hell as we walked through the parking lot. Why didn't I go over to the table and confront him? Well, why didn't I? I still ask myself that.

Her final words when we got to our cars were, "I can tell you this, girl, if that was my husband cheating on me, he would be walking funny a for long time then the bastard better have a good memory of all his pleasure when he was doing it with a whore like her or maybe it was one of those guys in drag from the Cinderella Club. I would make him feel some real pain. I told you I didn't like or trust that son of a bitch back when you were dating him. Call a lawyer."

As always, Anthony always had a good reason. He said she was one of the girls in the office who was having a bad time with her marriage and needed a friend to talk with. He felt sorry for her, he said. Another time I heard from a female bartender friend that he was drinking at her bar with a red head. I questioned him about that his pathetic story. He said she was some gal whose car had broken down on the Garden State Pkwy. He drove her to the nearest phone to call road service which happened to be a lounge. I couldn't keep his stories straight. He would look so sincere when he gave his lame excuses that I wanted to nominate him for the leading role as the Robin Hood for women of Garden State Parkway. But I'd had enough this time. I moved in with Sam for a couple of months, and then got myself an efficiency apartment near work. Oh, and I also got myself a divorce. I had so much ammunition against him that Anthony did not contest the settlement, which gave me half of our savings and the bedroom suite I had bought, plus a promise from him that he would never try to contact me again. Of all the promises he made to me, that's the only one he kept.

Whenever Sam thought I was getting on her case, she never failed to bring up my lousy marriage, adding "Didn't I tell you Anthony was wrong for you?" I know she wasn't trying to hurt me; she was just trying to make sure I would not get hurt. Finishing my scotch, I whispered "Goodnight, Sam" under my breath and headed for bed. It had been a long, confusing day, but not a bad one, all things considered.

Chapter 5

The next morning ended up being a great one for painting. I had one wall finished in no time, and decided it was time for a break. I opened my typical bachelor girl's fridge and eyed the contents. Ketchup, mustard and relish on the door, a half-dozen eggs, a milk carton with lipstick on the spout, half of a grapefruit, some orange juice, and a six-pack of Coke. I reached for the bottle of orange juice, took a long drink, put it back, noticing that there was a bottle of champagne in the vegetable bin.

The champagne was left over from one of my Friday nights with Sam. She had called, saying that she hoped I hadn't eaten yet because she was coming over with dinner. She came bearing two cans of chili and a chilled bottle of champagne. I convinced her a bottle of red wine would be more compatible. She thought the canned chili was just the height of hilarity. What was I expecting, she asked, pâté?

Payback can be delicious, and I had a good time getting back at her for that one. Knowing how she loved pasta, I invited her over for Italian food. She arrived all flush with anticipation of linguini with clam sauce, or perhaps a nice pesto. Instead, I opened up two cans of Spaghettios. Halfway through this haute cuisine dinner, we broke out into a fit of laughter. We took our bottle of wine and the glasses and went into the living room, where we sat on the floor by the coffee table. Sam reached into her purse and took out a pack of cheese crackers. As we shared the crackers, Sam said, "You may think you got me this time, but I heard about your cooking, so I brought these for on the way home."

I chuckled a little at the memory, then picked up the paintbrush and began painting the second wall and the frames to the kitchen doorway. It was about ten-thirty when I finished. I put the brush back down, thinking, "This looks damn good." I was surprised to find out that I was really getting into this painting thing. The kitchen was looking so good that I planned to start the living room.

Sometimes, even the best of intentions are waylaid. In my case, it always seems to be the phone that does the waylaying. Just as I started toward the living room, the phone rang. I thought that whoever was on the other end of the phone better have a damn good reason for calling. Sometimes I think Sam must be psychic; it was almost like just thinking about her a few minutes earlier had prompted her to call.

"Harry left early to go fishing," she said. "How about you meet me at the train station in one hour? We'll go to the city, spend the afternoon walking around the Village. We can get something to eat at O'Henry's; I know how much you love their Reuben sandwiches. By the way—you're going to like this part—lunch is on me. Then let's go window shopping in the village, New York is great on a Sunday afternoon." So much for my painting plans. I cleaned up the brushes, looked around at the mess of my house, and decided it could wait until later. I put on a pair of white slacks, a tank top, slapped on a little makeup and ran out the door to meet Sam at the station.

I couldn't help but wonder why Sam was being so nice to me, first the compliment on my outfit the night before, and now she was springing for lunch. She is always broke, which I don't understand, because she could give the word "frugal" a new meaning. We always go "Dutch." When we were in a cab heading to the Village, Sam turned to me, and her hand went up to her left ear which she was now tugging with a serious motion.

"Now I know I am in deep shit," I groaned. "Come on, Sam spit it out. I know this is something I am not going to want to hear."

"Well there you go," she replied. "What is it with you always thinking I am up to something?" She peeked out of the corner of her eye at me, than laughed. "Well, maybe I am. But really, it's not so awful. You know how my mother has been asking me for months to have lunch with her? I was think-ing how nice it would be for you to join us."

She sneaked another look at me, than grabbed my hand. "Oh, you're upset. I can tell. Your neck is all red. Say something!" She must have noticed my expression, because then she said, "No, on second thought, forget I said that."

The cab slowed to a stop and eased over toward the curb. "Well here we are," she said brightly. "No, put your money away. I'll pay the cab fare." She fumbled in her purse for a minute, than looked up at me sheepishly. "Do you have two dollars for the tip?" she asked?

Prayer is a good thing. I paused on the curb, praying that I could hold off on thinking about killing Sam until after lunch. We pushed through the doors and peered around in the dim restaurant until we spotted Sam's mother already at a table. She was taking a sip from her Gibson as we walked up to the table. Sam and I sat down and ordered chardonnay from the waiter who was hovering nearby. Looking over my wine glass, I observed Sam's mother as she took dainty sips of her drink. Dressed in a beige linen sleeveless dress with her jacket folded neatly on the chair next to her, she looked almost regal. She always was well-groomed, but today, with her hair in an elegant French twist, she made me feel that I should have gotten a formal invitation to dine in her presence. You'd never know by looking at her that she'd spent a good chunk of her life living in a bottle.

Chapter 6

Sam ordered her favorite lunch: a bowl of French onion soup and shrimp. I, of course, got my Reuben. I was curious what Sam's mother would order. It's unusual to see a woman with her strictly self disciplined poise eating in a Village restaurant. She spoke so softly in her Southern drawl that the waiter had to bend down to hear: "A small salad with fresh shrimp, fresh mushrooms, cherry tomatoes, and no dressing," she smiled "And I would just love another cocktail."

While mother and daughter conversed, I enjoyed my sandwich. I tried to ignore Sam's subtle distress signals: a flutter of the hands, with a swift kick to my shins. I just gave her my best "thank you for lunch" smile and continued chewing. Actually, the gathering was not as unpleasant as I had anticipated, considering we had two powerhouses, opinionated women seated side by side, neither one wanting to give the satisfaction of agreeing that the other may be right. The air around our table may have been a little thick with the tension, but I don't think it was contagious. Far as I could tell, all the other patrons were laughing and talking like normal people do.

Sam's mother had manners up the ass. She could eat with out hardly ever looking down. She would drop her eyes to spear something on her fork, raise the fork gracefully, and only open her mouth when the fork came in direct contact with it. After the food disappeared, she slowly lowered the fork to her plate, lifted her napkin, and dabbed at her mouth. This delicate ballet bore no resemblance to the roller derby approach she took to drinking her second Gibson.

Watching her eat, I felt like the three of us were having a high tea of tiny watercress sandwiches and vanilla wafers at Buckingham Palace. When Sam picked up the shrimp cocktail with her fingers and popped one into her mouth, the skin around her mother's eyes would tighten and her lips clenched so tight they almost turned blue. But really, Sam was doing pretty well, all things considered, until she lifted a large glob of cheese from her French onion soup on the spoon and proceeded to twist the other end on my fork.

"Here, girl, have some cheese," she said with a grin. Her mother glared and pulled her skin so tight I thought her face was ready to shatter. I swear, it looked like Sam and I were having a taffy pull. Sam was laughing like a kid who just put her pet frog in Mother's bubble bath. Half the fun of it for Sam was enjoying the fact that she was causing her mother to have a hissy fit.

"Mother, would you like to go window shopping with us after lunch?" Sam asked sweetly, as if she had no idea how upset her lack of etiquette was making her mother.

"I don't believe that's a good idea," her mother managed to squeeze out. "Maybe another time."

I kept waiting for Sam to mention something, anything, about getting married. I purposely dropped my napkin, and on the way down to retrieve it I whispered, "Tell Mommy about your wedding plans." Her response was to bring her hand down under the table and whack me on the arm.

Sam's mother asked me a few polite questions, just to let me know she wasn't ignoring someone she could really do without. I was starting to get some idea of how Christ felt at his last supper. Finally, the interminable lunch ended. Standing on the sidewalk, Mommy and Sam gave the other one the polite kiss that lands in midair. As Sam's mother floated toward a cab, she remembered that I was standing there on the sidewalk. I guess her manners dictated that she acknowledges me somehow, and she lifted one finger to wave. On second thought, maybe it wasn't a wave. My stomach was full, I had my best friend by my side, and an afternoon of window shopping beckoned. I decided I could get over the slight.

We strolled down the sidewalk looking into the shop windows and pointing out the interesting finds we would buy if we only had the money. As we walked by one shop, Sam stopped short and grabbed my arm. "We must go in this one," she said. "It's where I bought the muumuu last year, the one I had on last night. The fellow that owns this boutique is Hawaiian, a really good-looking guy. He designs a lot of the dresses," she said, trailing off with a dreamy look in her eye. "Look at that one in the lavender, and would you look at that one with the spaghetti straps, and the short one with white top and black bottom."

"You wear that and you'll surely be attacked," I told Sam.

She threw her head back and laughed. "God, girl, I hope you're right," she said.

The back of the store was mostly long dresses. To the right were shawls, scarves, racks of odd designs on thin leather straps you could put around your neck, and racks of chains. Then came a section of leather sandals. Just as we were starting to check out the sandals, the most unusual but striking-looking woman I had ever seen pushed her way through a maze of multicolored beads hanging from a curtain rod. She headed in my direction, asking if she could help us.

Chapter 7

She had light brown skin and long, straight black hair, dark eyes, and high cheek bones to die for. Over her arm were three hangers with dresses. I told her that I was just looking. Noticing Sam pulling a black-and-white dress from its hanger, I said, "But it looks like my friend could use some assistance." I picked up a pair of sandals, looked at the price tag, thought about my last bank statement, and said to myself, "Self, this would just about blow your budget to buy food for two weeks."

Then I heard a voice behind me say that the sandals were fifty percent off. Now this voice got my attention. I looked up and saw a very engaging smile coming from the dark tan face of a rather handsome man wearing white deck shoes, a pair of hip-huggers light weight denim slacks with bell bottoms like sailor pants, and a shirt to match tied at the waist.

Introducing himself as Corb, the owner of this fine establishment, he then went behind the counter to the gal who was arranging some jewelry pieces on a stand. He looked back up at me, then glanced over my shoulder and spotted Sam.

Maybe he sensed that the one thing that could

overcome Sam's frugality was a really nice outfit, maybe he was just a sucker for a pretty customer, or maybe he remembered her buying the muumuu last time she was in the store. Whatever prompted him, he bee lined over to her.

"How are you today, lovely lady?" he said, taking her hand and planting a kiss on it. She ended up deserving the special attention, buying the ankle-length lavender muumuu, one of the wide chains to wear around the waist, plus the black-and-white dress. I bought the sandals; hey, they were on sale. So I would eat bologna sandwiches for a few days. As we left the store, I realized that Sam had gotten to know the proprietor better than I thought she had. As the door clinked shut behind us, she asked me if I would like to go to Corbin's place in the Village in about two hours for a cheese-and-wine bash. It was now getting close to six, which would mean the party wouldn't begin until eight. And tomorrow was a work day. "Naw," I replied.

The train coming back from New York was really crowded, so we ended up in separate seats. I was going to bring up our Saturday afternoon phone conversation, specifically Harry's proposal of marriage in the tub of bubbles. I was thinking about it for more than twenty-four hours now, naturally I was curious to find out if her answer of "why not?" was a "yes" or what. Was she really getting married, or was she pulling my leg? Her silence on the matter made me wonder all the more.

On second thought, I figured; why not make her squirm by not saying anything. She must be just waiting for me to say something about it. Still, it seems strange. If she really were getting married, wouldn't the lunch have been the perfect time to drop the bomb on her mother? It would have been so like Sam to have me there for a buffer when she told her, just in case her dear old Mommy blew like a great white whale, spouting Gibson's instead of seawater. If she were just joking around, then this was going on too long. It was starting to feel cruel, and I was getting madder and madder as I sat and stewed.

Chapter 8

By the time we reached our stop in New Jersey, I had finally reached the tip of the pissed-off pyramid. Sam was without a doubt the most incredibly unpredictable, calculating woman a person such as myself could have as a friend.

The capper was when she had the nerve to say, as we came up the walk to my house, "You know, Megan, you have to get out and about more. How will you meet anyone?" That did it.

"Let me tell you, Samantha. How the hell can anyone call me? Every time I answer the phone, you're at the other end. Tell me how I could have anyone coming over when you are always coming over with a super major problem. Tell me how I can get out without you tagging along? I am glad you're getting married to Harry in some hick town I never heard of." I was so angry I was almost panting. She was in danger of assault from a deadly weapon, mainly my new sandals. We stood glaring at each other.

Chapter 9

Just then my next-door neighbors, a nice, middle-aged couple named Ceil and Max, came over and greeted us. They had been out enjoying the cooler evening air. Civility restored, we chatted for a few minutes, then they left.

I never could stay mad at Sam for long. Standing by our cars, Sam started laughing.

"What's so funny?" I asked, trying to remember being mad at her and utterly failing, which is what she knew would happen. As always I was the one who would give in.

"Remember the time I was over at your place? It was a Friday night, and we were having a glass of wine when the doorbell rang. When you opened the door, there was Ceil asking if she could borrow some instant coffee, like maybe you would give her enough for three cups. You went to the kitchen to look through the cabinet while we listened to her go on and on about her grandchildren?"

"Yes, Sam, I remember that only too well. I also remember what you did to me while I was putting stuff back in the cabinet," I said, trying to sound gruff through the grin I was struggling to suppress. "Ceil, said to me, 'It is no wonder you are so thin.'

Then she pointed to the large plastic board that sticks to the door of my frig like a flea on a dog.

Sam broke in. "Yeah, but instead of your usual grocery list, I wrote in big, bold letters: CARTON CIGARETTES, QUART VODKA, CONDOMS."

I snorted, remembering Ceil rushing out the door as her face turned beet red. Sam, was sitting on the top landing of my second floor steps laughing her self into a frenzy. She was actually holding her sides, tears coming from her eyes.

"Yes, I remember," I managed to gasp. "That's another thing about you, Sam. You have a very twisted, distorted sense of humor."

I turned back and opened my car door. "Hey, I have two packs of cigarettes in the car, and a half bottle of vodka in the fridge. Want to come to my place for a while?"

"That sounds good, but there's still something missing," Sam said. She rummaged through her purse intently, then triumphantly brandished her find: a box of condoms we both burst out laughing.

Mondays are bad enough without having a bodacious hangover. Maybe it was the combination of the martinis plus the pierogies filled with sauerkraut we ate cold that Ceil sent over the night before. I could not wait to pull into my driveway after a long, painful day at work. My plans for the evening were very simple: After my shower I was going straight to bed.

Then I heard a ringing in my ears. I shook my head to clear it, than realized it was the phone. I thought I had better answer. It could be the funeral director with the arrangements for Sam. She had called me at the office this morning, wanting me to be the first to know "she was sure she was going to die."

"Hi, it's me, Sam," she chirped, sounding much too lively for a dead woman. "I am calling you from ICU at the Betty Ford Clinic. They had to put me in a hammock, because I told them my bed was rolling around the room at a very high speed. Did I cheer you up? I hope you are feeling better. You sounded like hell on the phone this morning."

Before I could get a word in edgewise, she went on. "I threw up a couple of times, took three aspirin every two hours. Oops, when my head finally cleared enough that I could see the directions, I finally realized I read the directions wrong that I got it backwards: It said two aspirin every three hours. Oh well, I'm still here, so I guess that was okay. I drank a couple of cokes, threw up again, drank two Yoo Hoos, then ate a pack of cheese rings from the machine. That seemed to hold," she said. Without taking a breath, she continued, "Listen I want to tell you the plans for the wedding."

So there was really going to be a wedding after all. "Oh really," I said, trying to seem blasé about the whole thing, like she hadn't been driving me crazy ever since she mentioned it on Saturday and then refused to say anything else about it all weekend.

"Yeah, really. Like I told you Saturday, Harry and I are getting married in Macon."

Okay, I'd play along. "I never heard of Macon, New Jersey."

Sam laughed. "No, silly, a small rural area outside of Macon, Georgia."

Now she has my attention. Georgia's a long way from New Jersey, especially for a broke working gal like me. Plus, someone had to pay for the way I was feeling.

"Why are you getting married in a small rural area in a frigging place nobody has ever heard of? Why are you getting married at all? None of this makes sense to me whatsoever. You're marrying someone who's good under your hood and your sheets, okay. Fine. But let's see, you have been going with him what, two months?" I wrapped the phone cord around my hand, kneading the coils with my thumb. I took a deep breath, and then got into the heart of the matter.

"Sam, do you love Harry?" Nothing on the other end of the phone but her breathing. "Answer me, dam it, and let go of your ear. What you two are having is a kinky, totally outrageous, sexual affair, and that's great. But what happens when all the bubbles burst and the Sangria is all gone?"

"What is your problem? I thought you liked Harry. After all, you should be happy I am finally going to, as you always put it, 'settle down.' I certainly don't want to end up like some old maid that stands against her washer when it's running on the spin cycle." She sighed, and admitted that Harry and she had some of the same doubts. "But what else should happen after the Sangria is gone?" she said, brightening. "We'll be married, and we can always go buy some more wine."

Chapter 10

That's my Sam for you. She always sees the world a little differently than the rest of us. Who knows, maybe this unlikely marriage would end up working after all. And who am I to judge, really? It's not like my track record is all that great. I decided to just settle in and enjoy the planning. "So why Macon, of all places?" I asked.

"My grandparents, Memaw and Pepaw, are living there in a rest home, and they are not able to travel. So we figured we'd bring the wedding to them."

I said, "I didn't even know that your grandparents were still living," I said. "I know you've talked a lot about visiting them when you were a kid, but..." I trailed off. What was the point? She never seemed to want to discuss her family.

As usual, Sam brushed off my last comment and barreled ahead. "That's what I was just going to tell you. I just finished talking to them before calling you. They are so excited that everyone will be down there for the wedding and the reception."

"Sam, if I hear you right, you plan to have your wedding reception at the rest home?"

She said, "That's right. Memaw is seventy-nine

and Pepaw is eighty-two. I told Harry to call the Brunhilda who runs the home. I didn't want to talk with her. She's such a bitch to deal with, she probably wears leather underwear. Harry sweet-talked her into letting us use the dining room and kitchen facilities. Harry thinks it's a great idea."

"Well, that figures," was all I could think of to say.

"Memaw is looking forward to the reception. They are not certain whether they could come to the wedding because of their poor health—it would probably be too long a day for them. But the reception should be fine. Memaw is anxious for Harry and me to meet her two best friends, who are also staying at the home. They were Rockettes."

I said, "I always wondered what happened to the old Rockettes."

"No silly," she laughed. "Not the Radio City Music Hall Rockettes. These Rockettes were the cheerleading squad at Memaw's high school. The three of them were all Rockettes."

What could I say to that? "Oh really. How nice."

"Yes, and some of the retired musicians will play for us."

I said, "We must have a bad connection. Did you say tired musicians?"

"No, silly, retired," she said.

"Then Pepaw called his best buddy, Bert, to have him come to the church. Bert'd play the piano for us and sing 'Amazing Grace.' They always sing that at the weddings."

"Really? Sam, I always thought they only sang that in church and at funerals."

She said, "No, silly, but he can't come anyway because he's dead. Pepaw had not heard from him in years. Imagine inviting a friend to the wedding, only to find out that he's dead."

"Well, at least he has a good excuse for not showing up," I deadpanned. "Before you go on any more about these exciting wedding plans, could you please enlighten me as to when the joyous occasion is to take place?"

"Oh silly, everyone gets married on a Saturday, and we will too; Saturday three weeks from now. It'll be at exactly eleven thirty a.m. because they may have a funeral at ten-thirty, and then they keep the twelve-thirty open in case someone dies at the last minute."

I said, "Well, you could wait till after the twelve-thirty funeral so as not to rush the your wedding ceremony. Besides, how do they know who is going to die three weeks from now?"

"Oh silly, if they don't have a funeral scheduled for the afternoon, then they have the Saturday afternoon bingo game, like they usually do two times a month. The preacher calls the numbers, so he'll be busy. Folks come from all over; they look forward to a day out."

"Sam, I have never been further south than Asbury Park. Just where does one stay when they are down there in Macon?"

She said, "There is an air-cooled motel just a couple miles from the rest home and church. It's just down the road a piece either way."

Now July was hotter than hell at home, and "Oh silly" here was thinking Macon's a lot closer to the equator than New Jersey.

"What exactly does that mean, air cooled?" I asked hesitantly.

She said, "Oh, silly, you leave your windows open, and the ceiling fan air-cools the inside. The homes in the South all have ceiling fans. There is no such thing as air conditioning like up here. Besides, you will only be there a couple of days. It will be a nice experience for you."

I thought I could open all the windows in this house, turn on ten fans, and still sweat my buns off. This motel is down a dirt country road near the church. Down a dirt country road to the rest home. Same kind of road all these places are. Air-cooled with whatever comes from the ceiling fans did not float my boat, no way.

"Listen to me, Sam. If by some chance I call the airlines to get a flight down to where you arc having your wedding, just where do I tell them where I want to get off? You know, like, tell me where the hell is the closest airport to this motel/church/rest home?"

"You will have a problem with getting a plane down in that area. It's really all farm land. They don't have any airports except in Atlanta. I reckon that would be several hours from where we will be. How many I'm not sure."

"I really don't know about coming to your wedding, Sam, much as I would like to be there. First of all I can't take that much time off right now, and I don't think I can afford to fly, even if I could get from the airport to this God-forsaken place."

She said, "Oh, silly, why don't you drive down with me and Harry in his truck, just the three of us? We will have fun taking the trip together. My mother and father are going in their new Cadillac."
I said, "Why can't I go with your mother and father?"

"I think you should go with us. I know you would have a better time. I really would prefer that you forget about going with my parents. Besides, they may be bringing Sophie and Ralph with them."

Chapter 11

There it was again. Sam always tried to keep her parents separate from her friends. She never wanted to get into any discussion regarding them, and never invited them to any parties she had. That lunch in the Village was highly unusual for her, asking me to come along when she was meeting her mother. Now I understand why: Obviously, her mother must not be too excited about the idea of her daughter marrying a mechanic, but she would be much too well-bred to mention anything about it in front of me. But on a long drive, who knows what might be said?

Plus, if Sam's Aunt Sophie and Uncle Ralph were going along, well, that would make it totally an impossibility. Sam's father's sister Sophie, weighed a few ounces short of two hundred pounds on her five-foot-five frame, and she never went anywhere without a large cooler and bags of snacks. She always takes enough food to travel cross-country, even when she's just going around the block. Okay, so it looked like I was going to be stuck in a rental truck with the happy lovebirds. But why a rental truck? I asked her, thinking it odd that a mechanic wouldn't have a decent car on hand to drive down in.

"Because Memaw and Pepaw have some furniture they kept for us in a shed at a friend's house for when I got married. It's their bedroom set, a piano, and their dining room table and chairs. Guess what? You'll never believe this."

I said, "Try me."

"They're also giving us their old wooden ice box. Well, I am going to use that to keep my linens in just like Memaw did. In the South, they pass the furniture down from the oldest generation to the youngest. They don't buy new like folks up North. They figure if they buy the best the first time, why not keep it in the family, right?"

Someone was banging on my door. "Sam, I'll have to get back to you later. Someone's at the door, and if I don't get it soon, they're going to knock it right off its hinges." I hung up the phone and hurried toward the door, shouting, and "Hold on, I'm coming already." As I almost tripped over a paint can in my rush to the door, I was thinking that I would have to arrange a bridal shower for Sam. If I could manage to get the place painted and fixed up between now and then, I could invite some of the girls she works with at the office to come to my house next Friday after work. I guessed I'd have to get Sam's mother's phone number too—it wouldn't be right not to invite her, even though Sam probably wouldn't like it. Maybe her Aunt Sophie could give me the number?

I flung open the door to find Sophie standing on the top step, round and red-faced as a tomato in the late afternoon heat.

"Sophie! I was just thinking about you," I yelped. "Come on in." I grabbed her hand and led her over to the sofa, where she plopped herself down with sigh of relief.

"I plan to have a wedding shower next Friday for Sam. You know about Sam getting married, right?" I hardly waited for her nod before I rushed on. "Well, we only have three weeks before the wedding, and I thought this Friday would be a good time to have the shower. Instead of sending out invitations, being that everything's on such short notice, I thought to save time by calling everyone, starting with you. But now that you're here, I don't have to."

"Would you like to make up a menu of what you think would be nice to serve? You're such a good cook; I'd like to put you in charge of the food. Give me the bills for what you spend, of course. I'll call you by Wednesday at the latest—I should have the number of how many will be attending by then. Oh, and one more thing Sophie, I plan to call Sam's mother and invite her. Would you please give me her phone number?"

There was a brief silence, then Sophie said, "Your plans for a wedding shower sound excellent; however, I am not sure I should give you her mother's phone number. I certainly wouldn't want to do anything that would upset Sam. Perhaps it would be better if you would ask Sam if she wants to give you the number or how she would feel about her Mother coming to her shower. I would not do the asking myself without Sam's approval."

Okay then. Looked like I'd have to go to the horse's mouth for that one. I let it slide, and we talked about the menu for a while. My hangover was dissipating finally, and I could talk about food without feeling like I'd throw up all over my ugly green living room walls. Earlier, just the color of the walls was enough to make me feel queasy.

Chapter 12

Sophie finally left, and I began to make myself a shrimp salad and a hair of the dog—in the form of a nice cool glass of chardonnay—and thought over what Sophie had to say. It seemed a little out of character for her to be so stiffly formal with me about getting Sam's mother's number. But then again, there was something a little strange about Sam's family, both in good and in bad ways. I could only hope that, for Sam's sake, her marriage would be as solid as her Aunt Sophie's.

Aunt Sophie first met Ralph when she came up from her home in Georgia to visit her brother, Sam's father, when they lived in Bayonne. Ralph lived next door with his parents. While he had dated a number of women, he had never married. Ralph's not handsome, but he's not a bad-looking guy, about five-eleven, just a bit on the stocky side but not fat. He liked to play pool, and he was no slave to fashion. As he liked to say, "If it's clean, you wear it." When Sophie came to visit her brother for the first time, he had invited Ralph over for a cookout. The second time Sophie came to visit for a week; Ralph called and asked her out to dinner. Another night, he invited her to a movie and ice cream, and he asked her when she would be coming up again. The third time she came to see her brother was the last time. Ralph took Sophie for Chinese food. When the waitress handed them the fortune cookies, Ralph opened his. He told her his fortune said that Sophie was going to marry him. He handed her a ring and that was that. She never went back home again.

Ralph loved to work with his roses. He liked to boast that he nurtured them himself. The first time I was invited to their home for dinner, I at first thought he was very quiet. After spending some time with him, I realized he was very humorous in a dry way. Like when Sophie said, "When we were married, I was as thin as a stick." Under his breath, I heard Ralph say, "Yeah, now she's a redwood."

I was having a glass of wine in the kitchen with Sophie before dinner. She opened the oven and took out a roasting pan that held a meatloaf you could have launched. I said, "Sophie, how many are you having for dinner?"

She said, "Just four. Sam will be joining us in about a half an hour."

After dinner, which was excellent, Sam told me to go outside with Ralph and see the roses. She would help Sophie clean up.

Sophie cleaned off the table, and then made dinners for Sam and me to take home. From the living room. Ralph said, "Take it all or I'll eat meatloaf for a week."

Sam was helping Sophie get the dishes cleaned up and put away, so I went outside to see the roses. There were rows and rows of small and large beautiful rosebushes. I have ever seen roses like Ralph's. He had many yellow roses, my absolute favorite, and so many in other colors that it almost looked like someone had taken a paintbrush to the garden. Ralph said that he converts the side porch into a miniature hot house in the winter, then splices different branches to start new plants and prays they will take. He looked into my eyes as he handed me a yellow rose, which I mentioned were my favorites, and said, "Sophie and I were never blessed with children, I have my roses to fuss over."

Then Ralph motioned I should follow him into the garage. He was proud of all the cabinets he had built; everything was methodically marked on the front of the drawers. There was one cabinet with a lock on it. He took out his key ring "Guess you wonder why I have a lock on this one."

I said, "Is that where you keep your money?" He laughed.

"No, my nuts."

"Your what?" I said. He opened the door and there on the middle shelf were many cans of assorted nuts: cashews, peanuts, mixed nuts, and macadamia nuts that a friend sent him from Hawaii.

Ralph opened a can of cashews and passed them to me. I declined, being too full of meatloaf, but said that I would perhaps like some another time. He took a handful and put them in his pocket, closed the can and put it back in its proper place, then closed the door and locked it.

I could not help but wonder why he would have his nuts under lock and key. Seeing my curious look, Ralph started to laugh and said, "I guess you are wondering why I lock them in here."

I said, "The thought did cross my mind. Ten cans of assorted nuts locked in the garage does seem rather strange, but I guess you can keep your nuts wherever it makes you happy."

"Well, Sophie does not want me to have them because of my high cholesterol. I know she worries about me, but what's a few nuts? She thinks making pies and cakes every night for desert is healthy. When I die and she finds my stash, she will be mad as hell."

I said, "At least you won't have to hear her yelling."

"Don't you bet on that," he shot back. Then he pointed to his nose and said Sophie broke it over peanuts a couple of years ago. He was watching a football game, eating peanuts. It seems one got caught in his throat and he was seriously choking. Sophie came up behind him and hit him so hard on the back that he flew off his chair and hit his nose on the coffee table.

He snorted a laugh, than started in with another tale. "I was not Sophie's mother's choice; that was a fellow named Fred. When she would visit, she made a point of putting in a few sly remarks about how well Fred was doing. Fred took over his father's butcher store and expanded it, and he was doing pretty well for himself. One time, after Sophie and I'd been married a couple of years, she came over and just went on and on about the big house Fred had just purchased that had hardwood floors, and the new Cadillac he had just bought for his wife well, you get the idea.

"When she left, I just said, 'Sophie, I am sick and tired of your mother talking about Fred. You never say anything to her; you just let her go on and on about that ding bat, Fred.'

"Sophie said, you know how she is. Why don't you just learn to ignore her"?

"I made some sarcastic remark about her mother, and Sophie got furious at me. She raised her hand to slap me, saying, 'Don't you talk about my mother like that or mention anyone else in my family.'

"I said, 'Soph (she hates that name), if you hit me, I am leaving."

With that she just looked at me. Then she started laughing and laughing. I was laughing with her, and before you know it, it became funnier than a rubber crutch. It's good we both had better bladders than we do now." He chuckled a little, remembering.

I said, "You and Sophie are lucky. You've had many years together, and you seem to get along so well. You two have a love that others would envy, a friendship, and a deep respect."

He sat down on the bench. I sat next to him and he put a few more cashews in his mouth and said, "One day a few months ago Sophie said to me, 'Ralph, are we still in love?' She comes out with some dillies. I told her yes, but now we are also the best of friends. Over the years Sophie had her secrets and I had mine. For instance, we went to see the movie with Susan Hayward and John Gavin many years ago. I was sitting in the theater thinking that if John Gavin has the same effect on Sophie that Susan Hayward has on me; we would get to bed early that night."

He stopped chewing and threw a few more in his mouth. He said, "You know, many times a husband does not give his wife enough credit, like what she is doing is not important. Men are not as difficult to understand. We all think pretty much the same thoughts. We sneak looks at younger women or gals on the beach. We have our thoughts and fantasies. We don't ever stop to think that the women next to us, our wives, are more than likely doing the same thing, and rightfully so. But women don't make a big woof about it. Women are cool and mysterious;

they tend to keep their fantasies inside. That's what makes them special. I know I hide my nuts from Sophie, but she doesn't know I found her boxes of candy behind the cereal boxes a long time ago. That is one of her secrets and it will stay that way."

"Ralph," I replied, "like you say, everyone has their secrets and things they keep inside. We all have our own hiding places for our thoughts—some good, some not so good. I sure do have mine. As you know, I did not have a good track record for picking a husband, there is a lot with that I don't talk about. I am almost scared to get emotionally involved again for fear I may have a repeat performance. I have never talked to Sam about these things and I consider her my best friend but some times she gets on my case about finding some one again and getting married. Perhaps having children. That's what she should be doing but you know honestly Ralph I really think she is more scared than I am. She plays the field, meets some really nice guys, when they get down to asking the big question she takes off. Some times I think something happened that she does not want to talk about back some where when she was much younger, thank goodness she didn't hear that part.

We can be sitting around having a glass of wine. I ask her about her teen life and her parents, it's like she goes ballastic and shuts down. There is something she will not release not even to me. One time she came close by saying her Mother goes to bed with Jack Daniels and her Father would never make the Father of the Year and she speaks of him and you can hear the resentment in her voice. Maybe that's why she does not want to get involved. Maybe I am wrong about Harry. He could be the answer to her happiness. I may have misjudged what kind of man it would take to fill her needs and make her happy

I often wonder what secrets Sam keeps hidden," I mused. "We've talked about almost everything there is in our nightly visits. She never talks about her parents, or what it was like growing up. If I bring it up, she puts a quick end to it. I wonder why it is that a girl like that, who has had so many opportunities to get married, always breaks it off when the time gets too close. I know she's got her secrets too. I just wish she'd share them with me sometime."

Ralph looked at me and said, "There are some things better left unspoken. There are some things even Sophie won't talk with me about, some family secrets that she keeps close to the vest. I believe this fellow Harry has whatever it is that Sam needs and wants in a man. At least I hope so. I pray every night it's true."

Just then Sophie called us in for dessert. Before we went inside I said, "Ralph, you are a special man."

Sophie had made a dessert that was so good, Sam called it lethal: hot homemade peach cobbler. We're talking fresh peaches, not canned, with real whipped cream, of course. Ralph said he just wanted a small piece.

When Ralph left the kitchen, Sophie said, "My peach cobbler has always been his favorite dessert." She winked in my direction. "Guess he must of had too many nuts."

Chapter 13

I was just getting ready for bed when the phone rang. Big surprise: It was Sam again. She had more plans she did not get a chance to tell me about earlier.

I barely had a chance to say hello when she started in. "Guess what?" she said. "My great Aunt Bernice in Georgia, well, her Labrador gave birth three months ago and she saved one of the puppies to give me as a wedding present."

I said, "Isn't that nice. How is this Labrador getting back to New Jersey?" I had visions of puppy pee all over my pants, steam rising as we made the long, hot drive back to New Jersey. Not a pretty vision at all.

But Sam, as usual playing her greatest role, making everything sound like it was a perfect idea. Of course this way you could be assured that nothing could possibly go wrong. She had it all planned out. "My honey, Harry, had a great idea. He can hook his pickup truck to the back of the rental truck for the drive down, and then you could drive the pickup truck back to New Jersey. We can go back in the rental truck, with Blaze—did I tell you we already had named him—would of course sit in the front seat." Oh great, now I was being replaced by a Labrador.

She also thought it would be a good idea if we left a few days early, like maybe Tuesday, and stop in South Carolina to visit with her old school chum, Betty Sue Ann, and her husband, Bubba. They were living with Betty Sue Ann's grandparents, tending their farm of collards and tobacco somewhere near Aynor. I asked if that was a city. Sam said, "No, silly, it is the name of a small town. The farm sets back on a country road about three miles from town. Bubba also started pig farming: eight females and one male. You only need one of those. I think the eight of them had like ten or twelve piglets each."

Even thinking about going back down South seemed to be bringing out the Southerner in Sam. "Y'all will love it. We'll spend a couple of days with them. I'll tell you straight out it gets very hot there, but there's no need to fret none or bitch to me about it when we get there. Like the hotel in Macon, it'll be air-cooled. They have ceiling fans in most of the rooms, and large windows in every room. In the afternoon they close all the shutters that helps to cool the house by keeping the heat out."

This whole thing was starting to sound like a horrible ordeal. I could feel myself starting to per-spire. I felt short of breath all of a sudden, and could not feel my pulse. "Can I call you back later?" I managed to gasp. "There's, uh, someone at the door." As I hung up, I thought that the more she told me, the worse this trip sounded. There is no way I am going. She may be my best friend, but I hate camping out, and this sounded close to something even worse than that. Pig farming, for God's sake. Our friendship might not survive the trip to the wedding. I finished my shrimp salad, gulped the last of my chardonnay, and called her back.

"Hi, Sam, this is 'Oh, silly' telling you I am not going. However, when you get back, I will take you and Harry for dinner. This is too short a notice. There is no way I can get this time off from work approved. Also, if we wait and celebrate it after the fact, I'll have time to get you a very special wedding gift."

Before she could begin to object, I figured it would be a perfect time to switch the subject to the plans I was making for a bridal shower for her. The thought of lots of nice presents ought to be a good distraction, I thought. I also wanted to tell her that I wanted to call and invite her mother. Although I would rather have been able to make the shower a surprise, time was too short to be able to pull that off. While she liked the shower idea, Sam let me know in no uncertain terms that she was not pleased about having her mother attend. All right, so I guess Mom wouldn't be coming after all. I just hoped she wouldn't find out about it and dislike me even more than she already seemed to for not inviting her. Anyway, it'd be a lot more fun without the Grand Dame around.

I decided to let Sophie off the hook for doing all the cooking, so I reserved a room for two hours with a catered buffet for twelve at a nice restaurant. Sam was positively glowing, and laughed and joked in her usual way with her friends from work, Sophie, and me. When it was time to leave the party Sophie and I helped carry the gifts to her car. All of a sudden, the bubbly, happy person we'd been enjoying for the past couple of hours disappeared. Sam stopped short, then put her arms around us and started to cry. I had never seen Sam cry before, but she really outdid herself, sobbing and clinging to us like lifelines. She managed to get control of herself after a few minutes, and, with no word of explanation as to what all the tears were about, hopped into her car, waved from her partially opened window, and drove away.

I looked at Sophie, and then made a gesture that was meant to mean, "What was that all about?"

Sophie looked at me with tears in her eyes and said, "That was about a woman, and the little girl that still lives inside her."

I thought I knew all about Sam's past, but maybe not. After all, she'd never mentioned the fact that her grandparents were still alive until she started talking about the wedding. I did know that Sam's parents moved to New Jersey when she was about seventeen years old. Sam's father had been transferred from a plant down South, in or near Macon, Georgia, I now would presume, to their new world of Bayonne, New Jersey. There was never a hint of anything sad from her early days, at least not from what Sam had told me. Sam told me several times of the wonderful summers she spent at her Memaw and Pepaw's farm, which for some reason I never tired of hearing about. She had a way of making me wish I could have been there.

As Sam tells it, they wouldn't see a soul all week at the farm. Then on Saturdays, Pepaw would hitch up the wagon and they would go into town and get groceries from the small store. Then they would go to the end of the street where a small hardware store was on the corner, and across from it was a feed store where they would go to get what they needed to feed the animals and the chickens, and to get seeds for planting.

They would take the eggs, homemade smoked sausages, hams, and whatever produce Memaw hadn't put up for the family to town to sell. Sam never stopped talking about the wonderful corn, tomatoes, butter beans, and the sweetest watermelons you could ever eat.

She always said, when she was feeling particularly nostalgic for the South, "Ain't never tasted any of those in the North which came near to what

Pepaw, growed." Memaw also would take her to the general store for some hard breakers and boiled peanuts on their Saturday outings. When I asked her what hard breakers were, she told me that they were golf ball, shaped candy with bubble gum inside.

Not all those Southern treats were quite as good in reality as they were in Sam's talking about them.

Sophie did bring some back boiled peanuts from one of her Southern visits. I tried them once, and let me tell you, I "ain't never" intend to ever have boiled peanuts again. What's a pleasure for some is not a pleasure to everyone, that's for sure.

Sundays sounded just as fine, according to Sam. Her, Memaw and Pepaw would put on their finest things that they kept hung outside on the long clotheslines so they smelled good when they put them on.

Memaw would get up Sunday morning while it was still dark, Sam said, to make fried chicken, biscuits, a couple of fruit pies, and a crock of tea that would be iced after church. They would have biscuits with homemade jam and cold milk or tea before hitching up the wagon for church.

They always had a simple breakfast because after church they had a feast. All the ladies would bring food which was, Sam said, "the likes of nothing you could ever beat": baked hams, roasted chickens, and large racks of barbecued spare ribs, fried chicken, butter beans, black-eye, peas, biscuits, collards, and rice. The desserts were fresh peach cobbler, pecan pies and sweet red watermelons.

It would turn into an all-day outing. The men would play cards, pitch horseshoes, and take their short breaks by having some grain alcohol from their small jugs—that was no problem, Sam said, because their horses knew the way home. The ladies would do their share of telling stories and work on their needlepoint.

Sam always shone with delight and happiness when she told these stories, which made me feel as though I were there, even while making me envy her because she actually was there and I wasn't.

I remember one time when she broke into a fit of laughter remembering the story of when she went to a fair, "the only fair she was ever at" as Sam put it.

A man jumped from a plane in a parachute, and everyone screamed, including Sam. Well, his chute opened and he came sailing down like a bird holding a sheet. She was beside herself, she said, and she thought about it for days. Finally, she decided to give it a try. Sam went into Pepaw's closet and took his best black umbrella—which also happened to be his only umbrella—and went to the barn.

She went up the steps of the barn to the top loft where the hay was stored. She headed to the one side where there was a small opening. She perched in the opening, opened Pepaw's best black umbrella, and jumped.

The umbrella went inside out and she landed on the side of the barn where they stacked the manure-filled hay that had been shoveled out from the cow and horse stalls. She flew down into the soft manure hay with a splat. As she was coming down, Memaw saw her from the kitchen window and let out one of her best screams.

Sam was covered with that soft, wet, recycled manure up to her neck, including her hair. Other than her vanity, however, she was unharmed. Even though she had destroyed Pepaw's, best umbrella, he just laughed until his big belly was doing a tango all by itself. He decided that her having to be scrubbed down many times with hard yellow soap and hosed off outside was punishment enough.

Chapter 14

Over the years, throughout our wine-drinking sessions and walks on the beach, Sam had told me so many stories about her fun-filled times with her grandparents, and the wonderful times with her Aunt Sophie and Uncle Ralph when they took her on vacations with them. She could not wait to spend Christmas together at their house, she said, because she loved spending time with Sophie baking cookies, going Christmas shopping, wrapping the gifts together, and hiding them from Ralph. She also had some great stories about how she would "help" Ralph trim the tree.

But for all her talk about her grandparents and other relatives, Sam would never talk about anything she shared with her parents, nor would she ever allow the conversation to go in that direction. She had a way of changing the subject so beautifully that you never even noticed most of the time that she never really answered your question. To get that good at it, she must have honed the skill with many years of practice.

Since, Sam, has been living in New Jersey, most of the memories we talk about in our endless conversations are shared ones. We have been such a

part of each others' lives. In fact, it was I who introduced Sam to Harry, the man that Sam is apparently going to marry. It's rather difficult to find a good
and honest mechanic—especially if you are female.

There were several places I went with some
need of car maintenance, and they all gave me different diagnoses and prices for a cure. Then my
dentist told me that he always takes his cars for
service to this guy named Harry. The next time I
needed some work done, I looked up Harry at his
small garage behind the bus station.

Harry was what a mechanic should be. He knew
exactly what the problem was and in no time had
my car running like a charm. The cost was half what
was previously quoted. Now that I think about it, I
should have snagged him for myself.

My car is the type that likes to break down fre-
quently and creatively, so Harry and I got to know
each other pretty well. While waiting for someone
to find a part, Harry told me about how his parents
had been killed in an auto accident when he was
sixteen. Needing to get away from the tragedy and
forge a new life, he lied about his age and enlisted
into the Navy. He was in the service about four
years, he told me, when he started going out with
one of the daughters of the owners of the rooming
house where he was staying. He said that they got
married; he started working at a gas station as a
mechanic, and then decided to start his own place

when the marriage went down the toilet, as he put it. I guess my Anthony had a female counterpart in his ex: seems she was cheating all the time. They never had children.

Seeing as how Sam's car was breaking down pretty regularly, I asked Harry if he could take on a new customer. More people seemed to be discovering him, and he was really starting to back up his workload. He said, "Not just anybody, but a friend of yours would be fine." Sam called me later that week and said she was having car problems. No big surprise there: The tin can of wrecks she was driving kept on stalling. I mentioned how good a mechanic this fellow Harry was where I take my car.

That's how Sam and Harry met under the hood of her piece-of-shit car. She called me after she returned from the garage, and I use that word loosely. The garage was small; well maybe it wasn't really so small, but it was hard to tell with all the junk he had stacked everywhere. Maybe he could fit in an eighteen wheeler if he cleaned out the hoods, bumpers, fenders, stacks of tires, empty cans, drums, food boxes from the past month, empty coffee cups, and stacks of Styrofoam cups. Harry, you might say, is a pack rat.

Sam said Harry told her that under the hood her car was a mess, and the outside wasn't any better. She said she told him that he had a lot of nerve, given the way his place looked. Sam's car was a scary place to be, though; even she couldn't deny that. She had thumbtacks holding up the lining of the roof, and she covered the floorboards with mats so you couldn't see the road through the cracks. When you would say anything about her car, though, she would just laugh. She actually loved driving around town in that coffee can. Seeing her rearview mirror laying on the front seat, I asked how could she drive without it. She answered that she didn't give a damn what was behind her; it's what's ahead that counts.

One of my favorite memories was the time Sam had to go to court. She said that she was shopping in Newark when she got back to the parking lot, her car wouldn't start. She managed to snag some poor, unsuspecting fellow to give her a push. Well, it seems that he pushed her clear out of the lot and through a red light. When a patrol car pulled her over and the cop gave her a ticket, Sam said "Now there is no way in hell I am paying this ticket because it isn't my fault." The cop disagreed. Sam, of course, was determined that she was in the right, and insisted on going to court to tell the judge the whole story. She was sure that once he heard her side, he would know she was innocent of these charges.

Despite my suggestion that she take a lawyer with her, she was sure she could handle it herself.

She promised to call me after the hearing the following evening at seven.

I was hoping for the judge's sake that she was the only case he had scheduled for night court...

Needless to say, I was more than anxious to hear how Sam handled her defense. I was on my third cup of coffee by the time she finally called at nine-thirty.

"Well, I went to court and the place was packed," she said. "I thought I was the only one who had an appointment at seven with his highness the judge. Would you believe they never even called me until eight-thirty.

"When it was finally my turn, I told the judge, 'I am not guilty. This fellow gave me a push and he pushed me through the red light.' The judge said, 'Young lady, while there's no real excuse for running a red light, yours is one of the best I've heard in a long time. I am sorry but you were seen crossing the intersection of Broad and Market streets on a red light by Officer Kelly, who is present here tonight. He saw you, there-fore I have to impose the fine. You have two choices: it's either twenty-five dollars, or get thirty days in jail. I have many more cases to hear tonight, so make up your mind.'"

She said that she'd take the money, of course. She said everyone waiting started laughing, which ticked the judge off. He raised himself up and looked down at her, saying, "Your attempt at humor will cost you another twenty-five dollars unless you pay your fine right now."

The whole thing just made me laugh until I thought I'd wet my britches. Once I calmed down, I asked her when she was going to get a decent car. After all, that wreck she was driving around in was dangerous.

After a moment of dead silence, she said, "Never. Memaw and Pepaw gave me this car when they went to the rest home ten years ago." Then I realized this car was a treasure to her.

Inevitably, when Sam left work a couple of days later, the car would not start. She called Harry, and he towed the car to his shop. When he was driving her home, he asked her to have dinner with him. The romance between Sam and her mechanic soon after became a full-blown happening.

As she later told me with much sparkle in her eyes, "Just think if Memaw and Pepaw had not given me their car; I would have never met Harry."

I have to admit, no matter how irritating Sam, may get and many times push those around her to the limit, her way of looking at life then turning unpleasant things around in such a way of making life the best thing that ever happened to her, like no body else I ever knew could do this…

Chapter 15

The Saturday after Sam's bridal shower was another hot one, and by noon it was so humid the air just hung over my yard like the breath of an old dog.

There was no way I was going to finish cutting the grass or pull weeds from around my tomato and pepper plants. My best idea was to have a cold drink and relax under the shade of my big old apple tree. There has never been a fence between my yard and the farm behind me. They have chickens, goats, and six milking cows, a few of which were sharing the shade of my tree's huge limbs. As I watched them laze around in the shade, I thought that there was no way I could ever have farm animals and chickens, and then use them for food. They would all die of old age.

I laid down on the lounge chair and looked up to the sky, thinking about Sam's wedding. That got me to thinking about other weddings I've been to, although it took a hard turn of mind to stay away from thinking about my own ill-conceived nuptial. It was too nice a day to bring myself down with that.

Instead, I thought back to a wedding of a family friend's daughter that I attended last year on a hazy Saturday much like that day. I accepted the wedding invitation right off the bat, and then had to consider those infamous last words: what to wear? My best formal outfit was a white dress, navy-and-white shoes, a navy straw hat with large brim, plus navy gloves. That would work just fine, except that no matter where I looked, I could not find the navy gloves. I tried on some white gloves, but they wouldn't work: they made me look like I was going into surgery. Then the idea hit me to get white gloves and dye them navy blue. This was my first dye job, and much to my surprise, they came out damn good. Still, I didn't want to overshadow the bride. Then I remembered just who the bride was, and I decided not to worry.

I mean, I hadn't seen the bride in a while, but I had watched this gal since she was in high school, and she had never had to worry about anyone wanting to take advantage of her because of her looks. It seemed that everything that could be misplaced on a teens face that was not pleasant to look at happened to Ashley. Her nose seemed too long. Her face was totally out of whack for poor Ashley. She had a bad case of acne, was very chubby, and was spoiled rotten to boot. Her father, a well-known and respected cardiologist in Short Hills, absolutely adored her, and there were some close to the family who had been known to whisper that it was too bad he wasn't a plastic surgeon so maybe he could help the poor child. Imagine my surprise when I saw the blushing bride: Ashley Sandra Stilman was lovely. I guess she must have been a late bloomer.

The wedding and reception were held outside on the lawn of the Stillman estate, an English Tudor mansion with acres of manicured grass, shrubs, flower beds, a swimming pool, and, but of course, tennis courts.

A huge white arbor was set up for the ceremonies, all covered with flowers. Large baskets of flowers lined both sides of the walk to the arbor. The vast lawn had tables and chairs with huge umbrellas shading them, plus a large outdoor bar with several handsome young men in tuxedos waiting for their work to begin. Would you believe the entire color scheme was navy and white? I fit into the setting extremely well.

Several limos were already parked on the street and the part of the yard that was roped off for that purpose. As I looked down the street, I could see many more coming. While I may have fit into the color scheme, my poor old Ford was certainly in a class by itself, parked next to all those stretches. Several vans with signs saying "caterers" on their side panels were going toward the back of the house.

The whole thing seemed like something you would see in a Hollywood movie set, I was thinking when I felt an arm snake around my shoulders. It was Ashley's father. He looked so handsome and distinguished with his salt-and-pepper hair and always well-trimmed figure wearing a gray tuxedo.

He said, "I am so happy you are here to share this joyous occasion with the family." I asked where his bride was, and he laughed. She had been helping Ashley get ready for the past four hours.

Just then a van pulled into the main driveway so he excused himself, saying, "The band has arrived, I must show them where to set up. I will see you later. Save me a dance."

I had never met the groom. As I turned toward the arbor I saw this attractive young man that seemed surrounded by several other young men and decided he had to be the lucky guy. A waiter sauntered up with a tray holding many glasses of champagne. I accepted the champagne being one of my favorite beverages. It was iced to perfection, which was a good thing, because I was really thirsty. I was also feeling somewhat anxious because I couldn't find Sam anywhere. She was going out with the bride's brother at the time. He had even given her a family heirloom ring, but that's a whole other story, and one that ended up disappointing his parents, who were certain that he and Sam would be wed. I could have told them otherwise, but it seemed wiser to just enjoy the day and keep my opinions to myself. Since Ashley did not have a sister, she felt her closeness with Sam made her the ideal choice for her maid of honor. Too bad they didn't end up

sisters through marriage, but the days of Sam's rela-
tionship with Ashley's brother were seriously num-
bered: They broke up within weeks of the wedding,
though Sam would never tell me why.

I'd just taken a quick sip when the Rabbi made
his appearance. There was a sound like a chime
ringing, and all the attention went to the arbor. We
were all asked to be seated in the many rows of
chairs that were lined on each side of the long car-
pet leading to the white flower-covered trestle. The
music started, and the bridesmaids started down the
aisle, followed by a small boy carrying a pillow and
a little girl carrying a long-stemmed rose.

The two mothers then strode down the aisle,
beaming. There was a pause, and then the band
played the wedding march as the newly lovely
Ashley started down the aisle on her father's arm.
She was radiant. Sam, the maid of honor, was right
behind them.

When Ashley's father lifted her veil to kiss her,
she put her arms around him and briefly held him.
Tears were streaming down my cheeks, it was so
moving. I glanced up at Sam, and saw that she was
sniffling too. I was really in awe when they placed
a cloth-wrapped glass on the ground and the groom
smashed it with his foot. That never happened at
any wedding I had attended previously. The wedding service was beautiful, and thankfully brief. I
went to a Russian wedding once that was so long; I
was wishing I had packed a lunch.

Once the ceremony was over, the waiters reappeared bearing trays of all kinds of canapés, all finger foods, which we all appreciated. Except that my fingers were covered with the beautiful navy gloves, which beside making me feel very warm, made it difficult to eat the hors d'oeuvres. I started to peel down one of the gloves, but it didn't seem to be coming off—all I could see was more navy blue.

Dear Lord, my hand had turned blue as well! The dye must have seeped onto my skin when my hands began perspiring. I quickly pulled the glove back up and took a peek at the other one, only to find that hand too, was the same shade of navy. Horrified, hot, and hungry, I made a dash for the nearest ladies room, which for the occasion was in one of the cabanas by the pool.

I was praying no one would be in there. God must have heard my prayer, because the place was empty. I whipped off the gloves and started to scrub my hands with the liquid soap and nail brush, but they did not get any lighter. This was a disaster for me. Just then I heard someone else enter the room.

I was desperately struggling to get the gloves up over my wet hands when I heard Ashley's voice. I quickly hid my hands behind my back.

"I saw you come in and you seemed very upset. Are you not feeling well?" she asked. I hesitated, thinking how awful a thing my blue hands would be to burden the bride with. She came over to me, swishing her long train behind her, and peered at my face. I started to laugh, almost brought my hand up to cover my mouth, and then caught myself just in time.

"I'll tell you why I'm here, but if you repeat it to anyone, I'll deny it," I said, bringing my half-gloved, blue hands out from behind my back. We both cracked up, and I tried to tell her my sad tale between gales of laughter.

"God," Ashley gasped, her face turning red. "I was afraid this would happen. I have to pee so bad, and now you've gone and made me laugh, I'm about to burst my bladder. And how on earth am I going to get into the john with this dress?" She waggled the train, and it almost looked like she was getting ready to start crossing her legs. The girl was in a bad way. I decided to put my problem aside for the moment and try to help her out with hers before she had a totally humiliating accident.

"Why not just take the dress off?" I suggested.

"Do you have any idea how long it took to get me into it?" she exclaimed. "No, we have to think of something else, and fast. This is your fault for making me laugh so hard, so hurry up and help me out here."

"How about I throw your train over my shoulder and you back into the stall? I'll back up with you," I suggested.

She said, "You're coming in there with me while I pee?"

"Can you think of another way? Ashley, I have enough on my mind right now deciding how I am going to get these hands back to their normal color. Whether you pee on the floor or in the sink is totally immaterial to me. While you're deciding, I'm going to try and scrub these blue hands one more time."

When I took off the gloves, we started another fit of laughter. Ashley said, "That does it. You throw the train over your shoulders and we will back into the john."

I said, "I don't think you should sit down; better make this a stand-up job."

The idea was going very well when the door opened. Sam came in. "Where's Ashley?" she asked. I said, "She is behind me." I was standing in the doorway of the stall holding the train over my shoulder, and being careful to keep my navy blue hands well covered.

Sam stopped at the door, looked back at us, and shook her head. "I don't know what the hell you're both doing, but I would suggest the bride gets her ass out front. A lot of people are waiting to give a toast, including the groom. And don't you forget your gloves. They're on the top of the sink.

"Don't worry, Sam. I have no intention of forgetting my gloves," I said. "In fact, I will save them in mothballs to wear at your wedding. Or maybe you can keep them in your hope chest?" But Sam had already wheeled around and slammed the door before I got the last word out.

The wedding and reception was as close to perfection as any bride could dream. My hands returned to their normal shade in two days, after a lot of soaking and some creams that the pharmacist recommended. Somehow, I couldn't imagine how Sam's wedding, should it actually come off, would compare to Ashley's. But I've learned my lesson— no dyeing the gloves this time around.

Chapter 16

I opened the lounge chair under the big old apple tree at the far end of my yard and was settling myself down with a glass of ice tea, my book, and lazily listened to the cows munching on the bales of hay the farmer had just set out for them. Then I heard a distant ringing from the house. I was positive that it was Sam. Should I just stay under this wonderful tree and think happy thoughts, or should I answer the phone and get crazy?

Whoever it was, they were not going to give up, I thought as the phone rang and rang. With a sigh I heaved myself up and went into the house to answer it.

"Hi, Sam," I said almost without thinking. But it wasn't Sam after all. It was my Great Aunt Annie, one of my all-time favorite people.

Annie lives in Pennsylvania, in a farming area called Intercourse. She's been married twice, and I would bet she's not long away from finding lucky husband number three. Her first husband, Elmer Hinnershits from Blue Balls, Pennsylvania, was the one who got her started in the antique business. He had converted a big old barn into a antique shop. He went around the country and counties as he would tell the story but we all knew he never went out of the state of Pennsylvania, and bought up all the old furniture, lamps, stoves, refrigerators, dishes, pots, pans, jars, you name it, and put it all in his barn. Tourists came from all over New York, New Jersey, Maryland, and beyond to buy his collection. He kept collecting, and they kept buying. Elmer passed on three years after he and Annie were wed. Annie had learned a lot about antiques and kept the business going.

She found that she needed some help, so Annie hired Andrew Tuttle, who applied in response to an ad she had put in the local paper. According to Annie, that fellow really knew his antiques. He would take the truck and spend days or weeks on the road buying old pieces, then wait for Annie's divine approval. They were soon courting. We were happy when Annie told us she was going to marry Andrew. He seemed like an easy-going fellow, who was the extreme opposite from Aunt Annie; when she was not pleased, believe me, you would know it.

She had a heart of gold, though, and would give you the shirt off her back if you needed it. But boy, you better need it, or don't even ask. No one in his or her right mind would try to take advantage of Annie; she was one part Mother Theresa, one part barracuda.

Aunt Annie and Andrew were making money like banshees. Then came one bad winter, when the snow and ice never seemed to let up. Andrew was coming back from the Pocono Mountain area; he was in a hurry to get home with a truck filled with antiques he had gotten for the barn. It was Friday and he and Annie were going out for dinner Saturday night to celebrate their sixth wedding anniversary.

The weather was getting nasty; the light rain was starting to turn into a glaze on the roads as dusk began to settle in. Those mountain roads were very steep and twisty, and the temperature was dropping as the sun went down. No one will ever know exactly how it happened. The best the highway patrol could figure, the truck Andrew was driving must have gone into a spin as he was coming down a sharp grade. As the road turned, he lost control on the icy road and hit a tree.

I never knew Aunt Annie to show her feelings—she generally had cast-iron will- power when it came to affection or tears she did however surprise all of us when she cried at the gravesite for Andrew. When we went to the house for the gathering after the funeral, she showed me the anniversary card and the gift he had gotten for her: a very old and lovely cameo pin. They had found it on the floor of the truck.

As they said at the funeral, Andrew was a good God-fearing man. He never asked for help, but he was always there when someone needed him.

Andrew was a charmer, which made him a great salesman. He had a way of complimenting the ladies who came into the antique barn that made it certain they would purchase something. When I asked her one time if she ever got jealous, she said no.

"I have never had reason to think Andrew would ever cheat on me," she said. "I told Andrew and the husband before him, if you ever think about cheating on me, just remember: I have a gun and a shovel, and I won't hesitate to use them both."

"Aunt Annie, what a great surprise," I said, picking up the phone. We exchanged the small chit-chat for a few moments, just catching up quickly for the months we missed not keeping in touch. I asked if she was still doing her crazy antics and scaring people with her abrupt and some what eccentric ways."

"People say I'm eccentric and a little crazy, but how could I survive in this business if I weren't," she said with a laugh. "Look at my way I have these country people almost giving away their old furniture, Tiffany lamps, dishes, etc., to get more modern pieces. Meanwhile, the big-city people and tourists are buying their castaways at ridiculous prices to put in their homes and apartments. One man from Chicago bought a dozen old glass milk bottles for two dollars apiece. I asked what he would do with them, and he said he was a florist and would put one rose with a piece of fern in each and sells them for twenty-five dollars."

Maybe she was eccentric. She could be both weird and crazy like a fox. For example, when she had to have her top teeth pulled, she had it done in the hospital. She told everyone she was having her gall bladder removed, and she said she did not want any visitors. Then she asked the dentist if he could put braces on her new top denture, so nobody would know they were false teeth.

"Hold on a sec, honey" Annie said. "I have a customer." The phone clunked on the countertop, and I could hear her talking in the background.

"Okay, honey, I'm back. I just sold a Tiffany lamp. So, will you be home next weekend? I plan on coming down with the truck. A couple down there are selling their home and want me to give them a price on all their antiques," she said.

"Sure, I'll be here. When you come, will you bring me a couple of your homemade shoe-fly pies? And, if you get to a farmer market before you leave, could you bring me some scrapple and a piece of ring bologna?"

"My pleasure," Annie said. "It'll be good to see family. I get lonely thinking about Andrew, we were so happy together." She sighed. "But I know he is peaceful now, and I shouldn't feel so bad." Her voice brightened. "Did I tell you that the undertaker stopped at the barn last week? He bought a lovely picture of little a girl sitting next to a fireplace with a puppy and kitten sleeping beside her. The picture was for his granddaughter's birthday, he said. When he was paying for the picture he asked me if I would consider having dinner with him. You know, his wife passed on about three years ago."

"Well, are you going to dinner with him?" I asked.

"Why not? I gave him a lot of business over the years, after all. And there's this new inn they opened nearby that I've been wanting to try. It's a fancy place for around here, with guest rooms, and a fussy dining room with linen tablecloths and nap-kins, a fireplace, and candles on the table. I told him we could try the new inn, but not this weekend, because I have other plans."

I could just picture her in the bib overalls she always wears when she's working in the antique barn. Between the overalls, the straw hat, and the yellow work shoes that tie up to the ankles, she makes quite a sight. That undertaker had seen her through two funerals, though, and when she was going out, Annie cleaned up real good.

I said, "Go for it, Annie! See you next weekend. Drive carefully, not too fast, and don't pick up any strange men along the roads." Like she'd listen to me. I knew I was blowing smoke in the wind. She would do just as she pleased.

I thought we were finished with the chatting when Annie said, "Honey, will you make my favorite dinner, the sauerkraut, mashed potatoes, and pork loin?" Now Annie hates sauerkraut with one exception: mine. She said that nobody makes it like me. "Why don't you sell your recipe to someone?" she's said to me many times. "You could make a fortune." I always told her that I would give it some serious thought. We chatted a bit more, and then said our good-byes.

Chapter 17

Late that night, I finally got the call I was expecting. Of course, Sam waited until I had finished my shower and was ready for bed before phoning me.

This time I knew it was Sam when the phone rang—who else would call me that late?

"Hi, Sam," I said, pulling on my pajamas and stifling a yawn.

"Would you go shopping with me to get my wedding dress?" she said in a rush, not stopping to greet me by name.

I said, "Sam, don't you think your mother would want to help you choose your dress?"

"I did call and ask her," Sam said in a really haughtily tone "Do you know what she said to me?" She slipped into that slightly blurry Southern accent of her mother's. "'Your father and I will pay for your dress and other expenses for your wedding, but there is no way on God's green earth I will go with you to shop for your dress. No one has that much time in this life to spare.' She said she could dress the entire Higgins family in the time it takes me to decide on one outfit. The Higgins family has ten children."

In the interest of getting some sleep that night, I finally agreed to go on this shopping safari, an agreement which I later lived to regret.

Chapter 18

When Sam stopped by to pick me up at 9:00 a.m., I noticed that she had her Aunt Sophie in the car, which meant that the first stop would have to be food-related. Sure enough, Aunt Sophie wanted breakfast, so we stopped at a coffee shop. Sam and I had coffee and shared an English muffin. Aunt Sophie had the full special.

We pulled into the first department store two hours later. I was walking through the store with Aunt Sophie, but Sam was so excited about finding a wedding gown that she raced ahead of us to the gown area. I told her to get one that she could wear more than one time. She found very little humor in my suggestion, but nothing I could say could spoil her excitement that day.

The store was designed so that one had to pass through the bathing suit department to get to almost anywhere else. Aunt Sophie tugged at my arm.

"Come with me," she said. "I want to take a look around a minute while we are here. I could use a new bathing suit."

We had just started thumbing through the racks when a saleswoman came toward us.

Aunt Sophie said, "I would like to see a bathing suit in my size."

The saleswoman looked at Sophie and said, "So would I," then walked off.

"That bitch," Sophie said, but nothing was going to deter Sophie when she was on a mission. She made the rounds of the racks, and finally pulled out this orange strapless suit that would never hold what Auntie intended to put inside, even if they did a liposuction on her with an industrial fire hose.

"What do you think?" she asked, draping the suit across her ample chest.

"Well, it's bright. It looks like you."

"Why don't you find Sam? She probably has something picked out by now and is waiting around to get our opinion. I will try this on and catch up with you."

Sam was tugging on the right sleeve of her first gown when I walked into the dressing room, I sat down then noticed that two gowns were on a chair next to me. Sam was intending to try on next. She did not look like a happy shopper. The salesgirl that was helping her zip up looked even worse. I was under the impression that this was not going well at all for either one of them.

While Sam and the salesgirl worked on zipping Sam into the gown, Aunt Sophie walked into the gown room looking like they put her through a car wash. She had been sweating profusely in the supreme effort and determination to get herself into that orange bathing suit. Observing that she had no bag of goodies with her, I asked her how it went.

"Well, first of all, the suit was made in Taiwan and you know how small and thin them people are. They never make sizes for full-figured women." I commiserated with her on the inconsiderate nature of skinny-peopled nations, and we watched Sam mow through the gowns.

Naturally, none of the what-seemed-like hundreds of gowns she tried on were quite right, so we headed back to the car to move on to the next part of our adventure. We must have gone through the entire gown inventory of at least six department stores, but I couldn't tell you for sure. I lost count after a while. Aunt Sophie had the right idea. After a while, she gave up on Sam, found a lounge to rest her aching back and whipped out a paperback book.

Now that's a sensible way to shop with Sam.

By three in the afternoon, my stomach was talking to me out loud. That coffee and English muffin for breakfast just weren't hanging in there any more. I finally dragged Sam away from a pile of taffeta and silk that once had been beautiful gowns neatly hung on hangers, gave a commiserating smile to the poor salesgirl, who looked to be on the verge of a breakdown, and told Sam in no uncertain terms that I'd had enough.

"First, I am going into the drugstore to get me some Band-Aids for the two throbbing blisters on the heels of my swollen, hot feet, then I am going to have something to eat," I insisted. Sam relented and followed me to the lounge, where we picked up Sophie. I had to keep pushing Sam, who was giving longing looks back into the gown department like a puppy after a bone, and Sophie, who was complaining loudly about just about everything you could imagine, just to get them out onto the street.

Armed with Band-Aids, we finally got to sit down in a lovely garden restaurant, where I proceeded to remove my sneakers and apply first aid to my blisters. Once she smelled the wonderful aroma of sizzling meat, Aunt Sophie quit griping and grabbed the menu.

After scanning it with intense concentration, she decided to order a cheeseburger with extra mayo, French fries, a piece of apple pie with ice cream, and a diet Coke. "I have to watch my sugar, you know," she explained. Sam and I put in our orders, and once the food came, there was no sound but our not-so-ladylike munching.

Wiping my mouth with a napkin and surveying the wreckage of our meal, I caught Sam's eye. I was really not looking forward to resuming the trek all over the world so Sam could reject another hundred perfectly good gowns.

"What are you looking for in a dress, anyway?" I asked. "We have covered every department store in town, and you tried on some lovely dresses. What the hell was wrong with them? I mean really girl, you had on at least four dresses that really looked great on you. What is your frigging problem? I know what the problem is: We're out of places to look."

She didn't even have the grace to look ashamed of herself. "Oh silly, I just want to check out one more place." Sophie and I rolled our eyes, but figured we could handle just one more place. Plus, the shops had to be closing soon, right? We paid the check and went back out into the late summer afternoon heat.

The springs of the car groaned as Sophie hefted herself into the back seat. I hopped in as well, and Sam turned the key in the ignition switch. Nothing. Not a sound. That piece-of-shit car she drove would not start, even though Harry had been slaving over it just the other day. The temperature by now was ninety-five degrees in the shade. Too bad there wasn't any shade in a parking lot.

Sam spied a fellow just getting into a small truck. She hustled over to him, put on her best "helpless female" look, and told him her car would not start in a way that suggested this was the very first time in her ownership of this poor excuse for a car that this had ever happened.

He walked back to the car with Sam and stuck his head under the hood. After much pulling on wires and staring at engine guts, he said the best he could do would be to try to jump-start the car for us. A few battery cables and some horrible grinding and cranking noises later, the engine sputtered to life and we were on the road again, heading to the last of the bridal shops on the list she held in her hot hand.

The shop of course, was closed, as we found after driving six miles to get there. Sam managed to come up with another name, however, and we went off to that store feeling as desperate as a cowboy trying to herd cats. Please, let this be the one, the place where Sam will find her Holy Grail. No such luck. She sort of liked one dress, but it needed alterations and would not be ready in time for the wedding. Now keep in mind these bridal shops are like five miles or more apart. Every time I climbed back into that so-called car of hers, I got very religious. I had a mantra I would mutter under my breath: "Please, God, let this piece of shit start."

I applied more Band-Aids, but my size nine sneakers were starting to feel like size fives. I found myself not really giving a rat ass if she ever got married, much less found a gown.

Sam finally took pity on Sophie and dropped her off at her house. Sophie was so grateful to get home that I thought she was going to sit down on the sidewalk and cry when she got out of the car. Sam started off in the direction of my house, and then suddenly veered off.

She slapped the steering wheel and said, "I made up my mind. I am going to get that three-quarter dress we saw in the first store."

After what seemed to be an eternity of looking at long gowns, she now wanted to go back to the very first store we looked in and get the dress she was sure she didn't want. She was happy. I sat very still in the back seat, planning her death.

We got back to the store just before it closed. Sam headed for the bridal department. I saw a rocking chair in the furniture section on the way and lowered myself carefully, almost in tears from the pain coming from my feet and the joy that this horror show was almost over. She was finally buying a dress!

Imagine my dismay, the feeling of impending doom that descended on me as I spotted her returning without any box, bag, or other likely gown container. I felt pains erupting like thunder across my chest. She got to my rocker and, with a look of panic that looked about to turn into tears said, "I forgot my charge cards and I only have twelve dollars in cash. Suppose they sell the dress before we could come back on Monday night?"

I arose with the strength and determination of a warrior going into a major battle for my life and said, "Sam, come with me."

I limped through the aisles, pulling Sam with me by her arm— not by her neck, which would have given me more satisfaction, but I restrained myself. I was determined. Woe to any who dared step in my way; I'd plow right through them. I marched up to the desk, whipped out my card, and said, "Put that dress on my charge right now, please."

Driving home, with the dress neatly wrapped and stashed in the trunk, Sam promised she'd give me a check to pay back.

"Sam, consider it your wedding present. Just get me home, before I do something very painful to you." I shut my eyes and leaned back against the ancient head -rest. I was beyond prayers now. I put myself into the hands of the divine universe and trusted that it would get me home. And it finally did.

I didn't say a word to her when I got out of the car, but just waved a feeble little wave, my hand fluttering like a bullet-torn flag after a heavy fire-fight. I fell in the door and pried off my sneakers. Five band-aids were adorning each foot. I limped to the bar, poured a scotch with a small splash of soda—very small, believe me—went into my bath-room uncorked a wonderful bottle of bath bubbles that I had received from a friend that I knew would spend a lot more money for bubbles than I would spend for lunch and ran water for the tub. While I was soaking my wounds, I made a promise to God that Sam now has one more significant other that would never go shopping with her again. Like her mother, next time I'd sit it out.

Chapter 19

Living in New Jersey in the late sixties is, I suppose, just as nice as living anywhere else. Life is still pretty sweet here, despite the war and the protests going on in other places. You have the freedom of walking downtown in the evening and taking in a movie or an ice cream sundae. You feel safe stopping for something to eat or meeting someone for drinks. You can leave your doors unlocked, and whatever you leave outside unchained or not bolted down will still be there in the morning. Bicycles are left on lawns, and lawnmowers are left behind the house. No one worries about being robbed, mugged assaulted or any other crime of the season when he or she goes out in the evening.

Thank goodness for Sam that she lives in safe times. She often would get home, hearing the phone ringing or being burdened with packages, she'd just leave the keys in the lock like I mean all night. She would leave her windows open all night in her first-floor apartment. One time, the maintenance man in her apartment building was doing some plumbing work under her sink. The wrench slipped, and he badly bruised his hand. Sam put an ice pack on his hand, gave him a couple of aspirin, and went into her bedroom to finish packing for a weekend trip. She took a shower, dressed, and found the maintenance man sound asleep on her sofa. She never woke him before she left.

Maybe it was growing up in the rural South that made her who she was. I remember one time close to her birthday when she called to tell me I could take her out to dinner instead of having to shop for something special for her. Seems there was this great Italian restaurant in East Orange she wanted to go to.

Sam was right. This restaurant was definitely something else, with red-checkered tablecloths and napkins, and two large, gold, water fountains on either side of the three steps that went down into the dining room. One was a girl with the water spray coming from a hole in each of her massive gold breasts; the other one was a small boy peeing a stream of water into a gold shell. Each table had the red checkered table cloths and napkins, the Chianti wine bottle holding burning candles; a fellow was playing an accordion and singing "That's Amore" with a heavy Italian accent. He kept circling the restaurant, making certain he came back to where we were seated several times. Sam was certain she had seen him working in the produce section of A&P.

The waiter poured our wine, than took our order. We both had the clams casino and veal parmesan. I lifted my wine glass and wished her a happy birthday. When I asked her how old she was, she just smiled and said, "I am one year older than when you asked me last year." I knew full well that she wouldn't give me a straight answer because she couldn't remember what age she gave me the last time I asked. I decided to have a little fun with her by asking her another trick question.

"Sam, what nationality are you?"

"Southern."

"I mean your ancestors, where are they from?"

"The South."

"You believe all Southern people are just that? That none of you are from Europe, or Africa, or Asia? Sam, are you telling me that all Southern people had their own Adam and Eve and just started from scratch and went on from there?"

"That's right," she said with an annoying little smile. "We came from angels' blessings just like every other baby, except our seeds did not get all mixed up before they were planted."

"Sam, you are beginning to irritate me."

"Before you get totally pissed off," she said sweetly, "would you order me a piece of cherry cheesecake with a candle?"

Chapter 20

Another time, I stopped by her place on a Saturday morning; Sam answered the door wearing a red-silk teddy with patent leather red shoes with three-inch heels

"Sorry, Sam," I said. "I thought you were alone."

"I am alone. Come in, I am doing my laundry."

Now this gal had legs that started under her armpits. Her five-foot-eight body just swayed atop them, moving like a stalking green-eyed cat. I checked around as I came through the door to make sure she wasn't joking with me. I didn't see any man things like the last surprise visit when I sat down on her sofa and pulled up from between the cushions a jock strap with red lip prints; when I showed them to Sam, she started to laugh then told me Harry thought she had lost them in the laundry.

"You actually wear that when you are doing laundry?" I said. "I would never think to dress that way to wash my clothing. I usually wear shorts and a tank top.

"No, silly, I just bought these red shoes on sale about two weeks ago during my lunch hour, and I want to break them in. Harry is taking me to that new place in Asbury Park for dinner and dancing. I want to be able to move," she said, swinging her arms and doing a pirouette. "By the way, don't call me until tomorrow night. I think I'll take this red teddy with me just in case I decide to wear something to sleep, pulling it over her head. "Better throw it in the suds."

Okay. "Hey, I have to go; by the way, here are your keys. You left them in the door all night again, way to go, girl."

She stuffed the red teddy into the machine, turned around to me with a big smile, looked back at me over her shoulder. "Y'all come back again now, yah hear?"

There's a lot of Southern in that gal.

Chapter 21

Finally, the wedding trip was ready to get underway. Sunday afternoon Sam called me and said that, since I was not going to be driving down with her and Harry, they were leaving Monday early so they could take their time meandering down to the wedding site, with a stop at Betty Sue Ann and Bubba's farm. She thanked me again for the dress, and I wished them both happiness, and a safe trip. I would have asked her to keep in touch, but why bother? The hounds of hell couldn't keep that girl away from a phone.

Sure enough, a couple of nights later I picked up the phone to hear Sam's voice. "Guess what happened?" she said excitedly.

"Okay, I'll bite. Sam, what happened?"

"We were close to South Carolina on Route 95 when Harry pulled over. He told me that he needed to sleep, but he couldn't all spread out on the seat. So he went back to his pickup truck to lay down, and I started driving the rental truck. About an hour later it started to shower, and the roads started to get wet. Just as I turned a curve on the highway, something broke loose in the hitch or whatever the hell you call it.

The pick up truck came loose and went down an embankment, with Harry still in it."

"Lord, have mercy," I said. "How is he?"

"He didn't break any bones or anything, but they want him spend another day in the hospital here because they want to X-ray his back and neck again just as a precaution, since he flew out the door. I think he landed on his shoulder. They said the hitch wasn't secured properly. He said he knew how to put on a hitch, but I guess he didn't.

"It was really funny," she said. "There was Harry lying in the ditch in just his underwear. He looked real hot, stripped to his shorts; you know the pair I got him for Valentine's Day with the red heart you know where. Anyway, a trucker stopped, then went to call for help. The trucker said he has seen a lot of strange things riding up and down this highway, but this has to be the damnedest thing he ever saw.

"If you want to call Sophie and Ralph about all this, that's fine. Just make certain you let them know we are fine and tell them not to mention any of this to my parents. I mean it, not a word, okay?"

I promised her I'd pass the news along, and asked her if they'd be able to get back on the road. Sam said that the truck just got some minor dents and scrapes but nothing Harry couldn't patch up when they got home.

The next evening Harry called to say he was doing well enough to be released in the morning.

The X-rays just showed muscle strain and contu-
sions that would take a few weeks to heal. He
should be fine for the wedding, he said. Sam would
come over early to get Harry checked out of the
hospital and get his prescriptions filled for the
aches and stiffness he may have driving down, and
then they planned to hit the road.

Sam said she'd call me later to report on the
progress of their trip. I suggested they stop over a
night and not push the driving straight through to
Betty Sue Ann's place, but Sam was determined to
keep driving until she arrived at her destination.
With her heavy foot, Sam would have made a good
race car driver: fast and fearless.

When the phone rang a couple of days later, I
knew it had to be Sam and Harry. Sure enough, they
had made it safe and sound to Betty Sue Ann and
Bubba's farm.

Harry said the grandparents went to Charleston
for a couple of days to visit some friends. "Thought
they would leave us 'youngins' alone a couple of
days," he said, adding that Sam was too tired to talk
right then because she did a lot of the driving, but
she wanted him to call because she knew I would
worry if I hadn't heard from her.

"She will call you back later," Harry said. "She
wants to get the food and stuff we bought on the
way down into the fridge before it goes bad. It's
been in the hot car for several hours now."

"Tell Sam to call me tomorrow night. I called Sophie and Ralph and followed her instructions that the message was to go no further. Listen, Harry, we're having a violent storm here with a lot of thunder and lightning. I better get off this phone before I get myself electrocuted."

The next day was a typical Monday, and I had a lousy day at work. I came out of the office building into a parking lot that had turned into an inferno. I wanted nothing so much as to get home, get out of my stockings, and relax with a cool bath.

The Parkway was backed up as usual, and I was straining at the bit to get out of the traffic and get myself home when I heard a whoop and felt a thump. That sound combination could only mean one thing: I had a flat tire. I pulled over and walked around the back of the car. Sure enough, the son of a bitch was flat.

I looked at the lines of cars going by, hoping the look of desperation on my face would impel someone to get out of his or her car and help me change the tire, but I didn't get any takers. Okay, so I had to figure how to do this thing myself. I popped the trunk and proceeded to get what looked like the jack; it had to be that crowbar thing, right? Then I struggled, sweating and cursing, to get the spare out from the trunk.

Just then a car pulled over and this massive man got out and came over to me with a great smile on his face. He was wearing a black T-shirt that had "moose" spelled out in white letters on the front. He took one look at the flat and said, "Well, lady, at least it's only flat on the bottom."

That kind of humor I did not need at the moment, thank you very much. But I needed all the help I could get, so I swallowed the impulse to tell the Moose where to go and dredged up a sickly grin. I asked him if he could help, and he went about the exchange of tires like it was second nature to him. When he was through, I handed him a $10 bill, all I had on me at the time. He thanked me but refused the offer. I was really grateful and told him his help was more than appreciated.

As he walked back to his car, he said, "Better stop at the gas station on the next exit ramp and get the air checked in that spare tire." He climbed into his car, gave a little wave, and pulled back into traffic.

I proceeded to close the trunk and, wiping the downpour of perspiration from my face, got into my car. I knew the next exit ramp was only two more miles. It certainly was not out of my way. I thought that I had better take his advice and have the air checked. The last thing I needed was to have to stop at six-thirty the next morning on the way to work to replace a tire.

I now had a hell of a headache, my entire outfit was drenched with sweat, and my feet were killing me, but I would stop at the station to get the air checked. Pulling off the ramp, I headed toward the station. I couldn't believe my eyes—my car was the only one in sight as I pulled over to the air pump. I could see a fellow behind the cash register, or at least I saw some movement. Maybe he would come out and help me. Just then I heard a familiar voice coming from inside the garage. "Be right there soon as I find the tire gauge," he said. Then who should come out of the dimness of the garage but my old friend, Moose.

"How many of you are there?" I asked with a smile.

He let out a voracious laugh. "Just one, darling, but that's all anyone could need." He checked all the tires, and then suggested that I leave the flat tire with him to patch up. I could pick it up in a couple of days. If he could not fix it, he said, he would sell me a new tire for a good price. Before he went to the trunk, he took change from his pocket, went to the soda machine, and came over with a bottle of Coke dripping with condensation.

"Here," he said, handing me the soda. "You look like you could use a cold drink."

"You are so right," I said, taking the bottle thankfully. "Do you think the tires are all right now that you checked them?"

He laughed. "They look fine to me. Should stay fine, unless they go flat."

That's fine with me, Moose, as long as you keep riding up and down the Parkway. I was thinking, now this guy I would not refuse if he asked me for a date. That idea was shot to hell when I noticed the gold band on his left hand. Oh well. While Sam and I may share in having car troubles, it didn't look like I'd get my mechanic in shining armor, like she got Harry.

Chapter 22

It was almost seven-thirty when I pulled off the Parkway and headed for home. That yogurt I had for lunch was long gone. I had no desire to make anything, so I stopped at the deli and had them make me corned beef on rye with a large pickle and box it to go.

Like the saying goes, be it ever so humble, there is no place like home. I crawled into the shower, ate a couple of aspirin, and put on shorts and a tank top. Feeling almost human again, I took my boxed dinner and a large glass of iced tea and went out on the patio.

What a view I had. One reason I had for buying this house was that no one would build behind me. There were several acres of farmland rolling off in the distance, and the family living there was friendly. I'd been inside their old-style country home many times, and loved the atmosphere in the place.

It had wide window sills, a big old fireplace in the living room with an overstuffed sofa and two chairs, along with a player piano with rolls of music. Their large front porch had a swing chained from the ceiling, and there were always a lot of cats sitting on the five steps that went up to the porch. A dozen or so cattle were grazing in the field by the old barn—two of them were males with bad attitudes who I knew to stay away from. There also were some goats and several young calves that had been born that spring. What more could you want than to have open country behind you, a nice supper in front of you, and a long, lazy evening to enjoy it?

My pleasant daydreams soon were shattered by the damn phone ringing. Sam.

"Sorry I'm calling so late," she said. "We had to take the wagon and go for father."

"What happened to him?" I asked, confused. "I thought Betty Sue Ann's parents were in Charleston visiting friends."

"No, silly. Not father. F-o-d-d-e-r."

"What the hell is fodder?"

"Up North they call it cow-feed. Down here, it's fodder."

"Oh," I said, feeling edified. I could smell the fodder from the farm in back right from my porch if the wind was blowing right.

Sam laughed "Oh, silly, you are truly a city girl, what you were smelling was "recycled" fodder."

Sam explained that they spread that in the fields where they grow the vegetables. It makes things grow bigger and better. Sam then gave me a short course that included the full update on the fertilization of fields and pastures, and how most of the pigs had recently given birth to least ten babies each. Two of Betty Sue Ann's cats had had kittens recently, and the dog was pregnant. The neighbor's horse that grazed in the adjoining field was catching wind of their prize mare, who was coming into season, and who knew what may come of that. Even Betty Sue Ann was expecting.

"You know, Sam, you better be careful. Sounds to me like you and Harry are in very fertile territory.

"Oh, silly, don't worry about that. I told you how bad Harry sprained his back in that accident; besides, he has spasms so he has to stay on his back to sleep."

"Who's talking about sleeping? Sam, listen to me very carefully," I said. "My momma didn't raise no fool: No man's back is ever too sore in the heat of the night."

They all had plans the next night to go to the town hall for shag dancing. I had no idea what that meant. Sam explained that the shag is a mix between flat foot and the jitterbug without a lot of bouncing. She said "she would teach me when she gets back."

"Not if I have anything to say about it," I snorted.

Sam said that Betty Sue Ann's grandparents have won many a shag contest. They timed their vacation so they'd be gone during the contest. They figured they would give another couple a chance to win the trophy this year.

Being curious, I asked what kind of trophy they gave the winners. Sam told me it was about six inches high and made of white plaster, with the words "Shag Trophy" printed on the front in red. Sam proceeded to tell me with great pride that her Memaw and Pepaw had won six shag trophies.

Sam said her Pepaw was the repeated trophy winner for the church horseshoe competition games as well. They have all their trophies with them at the nursing home and, if I would change my mind and come to the wedding, I would get to see this marvelous collection. She again reminded me how much I would miss by not coming to her wedding. I told her I knew it was going to be wonderful, but I still really just couldn't make it.

I woke up the next morning with a strange feeling. I think it was guilt. Actually, I was feeling lousy about not going to Georgia to share Sam's big day with her. But it was too far to drive by myself—especially with iffy tires. And Sam's parents were driving down with Sophie and Ralph, so it would not be possible to hitch a ride with them.

I sighed, and heaved myself out of bed. As I scurried around getting ready for work, though, I started feeling worse and worse about the whole situation. I was surprised when the phone rang, and even more surprised to find it was Sam's Aunt Sophie on the other end.

"Have you heard anything from Sam?" she asked. "I guess it's pretty quiet and dull not having her bugging you."

"Nothing since last night, Sophie," I said with a laugh. "It sounds like they're enjoying their visit with Betty Sue Ann and Bubba, and like they're staying out of trouble. At least for the time being."

But Sophie had something else on her mind than catching up with the Sam chronicles, I could tell. After a few minutes of small talk, she said, "Ralph and I were talking about driving down ourselves, which, to be honest with you, we would prefer over going down with Sam's mother and father. We plan to leave on Thursday morning, and we'd love it if you could take the time off and drive down with us.

We wouldn't really have to rush. We could stay overnight in South Carolina on Thursday then get to Macon on Friday and find a place to stay. Just think about how surprised Sam and Harry would be if you came to their wedding after all."

I said, "What about your plans to drive down with Sam's parents?"

It was quiet, and then Sophie said, "Well, they want to leave tomorrow, and then will visit everyone down there and we don't need to get there that soon. Besides, they plan to spend a few days after the wedding before coming back and Ralph cannot get that much time off his job. We want to save a weeks vacation for another trip."

Sounded reasonable, but I wasn't buying it. For some reason, they just didn't want to drive down with Sam's parents. I decided to play along, even though I really didn't have any intention of joining them.

"We could leave early Sunday morning after the wedding, stop overnight again in Charleston or up the road in another place in North Carolina, and be back home on Monday," Sophie continued.

The idea of only taking three days from work during the busy time seemed more feasible.

I could hear Ralph in the background saying, "Oh, come on, get yourself ready girl, and go with Sophie and me. You would make us both happy, and just imagine how happy you will make Sam on her big day."

They were working on the nerve ends of my guilt fibers; I finally could not take the sob story any longer. Even as I found myself agreeing, I was thinking, "Please, God, don't let me regret this."

I was going to a Georgia wedding! I grabbed my purse and ran out the door to get to work, thinking that I had a lot to do to get ready. Look out Macon, here I come.

Sophie's not known for being able to keep a secret, so I called her as soon as I got to my desk to warn her that when and if she spoke to Sam, there was no way she should give any hint that I was coming. She promised on Ralph's life that she would not give away the surprise. I thought, well, this would be a good test of what she thinks of Ralph.

The next two nights were spent in a flurry of packing, unpacking, and repacking. And yes, I did leave those blue-dyed gloves home this time.

It was hovering around five o'clock Thursday morning when Ralph and Sophie pulled into my driveway. They looked so awake and excited it bordered on disgusting. How in the world could they be so revoltingly chipper at such a ridiculous hour? Only two things should be up at this hour: God and roosters.

Ralph came around and opened the trunk of the car, then said, looking at my bags, "I'm glad you don't travel like Sophie." He lifted my suitcase and garment bag into what seemed the only space left in the trunk.

The trunk was consumed with Sophie's suitcases, Ralph's small case, many gifts, and Sophie's two pillows. She would never leave home without her pillows. Once my luggage was settled, Ralph made the sign of the cross and slammed down the lid. He smiled and gave a sigh of relief saying, "Well, that's a good omen. I was afraid I'd have to get Sophie out of the car to come sit on the trunk to get it shut." He grinned, and I grinned right back, his good humor beginning to infect me. "If all goes well, tonight you will be sleeping in South Carolina," he said, escorting me to the door of the car. "You will like Charleston, I am certain of that."

Ralph opened the car door for me, and I couldn't help but notice that it was a good thing I'm not a large person. Dear Sophie had more than half of the back seat piled with gift-wrapped boxes in assorted sizes, all with very large bows. The floor behind the driver's seat was completely taken up by a large cooler. Next to that was a large shopping bag that appeared to hold many bags of assorted snacks.

I settled in, making the best of the area allotted to me. I did wish, however, that they had left me a little more legroom. Sophie had the seat pushed back as far as she could to make room for her overnight case, a stack of those gossip papers she liked to read, and a purse that could double as a suitcase.

I decided to try to take a nap. Like so many other people, I can't sleep the night before I go away on a trip. I'm always afraid that maybe this time the alarm won't go off, or maybe it would and I just wouldn't hear it. The night before, I woke almost every hour and lay there, eyes wide open, doing mental packing rechecks to make sure that I didn't forget anything. I even got up twice to check that all plugs were pulled on the TV and coffee maker, and to make sure the pendulum clock was stopped.

As I crunched myself into a ball and lay half-snoozing in the back, I could hear the comforting buzz of Ralph and Sophie making small talk about how heavy the traffic was, how they were looking forward to seeing Sam get married, and how it was just too bad that Sam and Harry could not drive down with the three of us. They talked about Sam like she was their daughter. "Just think, Ralph," I heard Sophie say, "In a few days we will see her again. That's the important thing."

I could not help but think that it was a good thing Sam and Harry weren't with us, because there was barely room for me in that back seat. We would have needed to rent a bus. But still, I would have really liked that idea of having them in the car with us myself to liven things up a little. I almost reached for the book I brought with me to while away the hours, but it was just too early to start reading. I laid my head back and listened to two dear people discussing the next several days. I must have dozed off eventually, because I came to with a start when I felt Sophie tap my leg. "It's pit-stop time. Come on, get out."

I looked around blearily, but had no idea where we were until Sophie informed me that we were in Virginia. So far, it didn't look all that different from New Jersey to me.

Sophie and I went into the roadside convenience store. She got directions to the ladies room. I bought a cup of coffee and walked around the store. The girl behind the counter was having a nasty time with the register. She apparently was new, and it looked like the register was fighting her, refusing to open the drawer no matter what key she pushed. The four impatient customers waiting in line, anxious to get on the road again and making comments weren't helping. Ralph came in to pay for the gas and saw her dilemma. He reached over the counter and pushed something, and the drawer popped open with a "ding." She smiled gratefully at him, then turned back to help the next customer.

Ralph and I waited inside the store for Sophie, rather than outside in the heat. I picked up a pack of cheese crackers, but Ralph told me not to eat that junk. "There's so much food in the car. Why don't you wait, and we'll have something when we leave here."

"Ralph that may be easy for you to say, you probably had breakfast. But I certainly didn't— there's no way I could face even trying to cook at four a.m."

"Well, honey," he said, scratching his chin, "I packed the car last night and we went to bed early. Sophie and I got up this morning at four and had French toast with bacon, finished a cantaloupe so it would not spoil while we were gone, then split a

Danish. If I'd have known you wouldn't have breakfast before we left, we could have brung you over
and fed you, too." He spotted Sophie returning from
the ladies' room, and we pushed back out into the
heat that shimmered over the pavement.

When we got back in the car, I opened the cooler to reconnoiter. I took out a sandwich bag, which
said in big, black letters that it contained roast beef
on rye. There was a tag Scotch-taped to the waxed
paper that informed me it didn't have any seeds. I
had to laugh because, much as I like rye, I will not
eat any bread or rolls with seeds. I found another
bag with packets marked "mayonnaise," "mustard,"
"ketchup," and "relish." I put my opened Coke bottle between my knees, put my sandwich on a paper
plate, and then went into the chest again to look for
pickles. And found them.

"Have you ever forgotten to pack anything,
Sophie?"

She laughed and said, "Just one time. I forgot to
bring toilet paper." She glanced back and saw my
questioning look. "When you are on the road, you
may find that some gas stations or rest areas don't
have any toilet paper. Now that's one thing you
never want to be without. I have three rolls tucked
under the back seat," she said. I checked: Believe
me, she was not kidding.

The second layer of the cooler contained ham
and Swiss cheese sandwiches on pumpernickel, and

turkey breast on her homemade bread. There was a plastic container of pickles, a jar of olives, a plastic tray of cut-up cheese, soda, juices, plus a tray with deviled eggs. In addition, she had stashed brown store bags with chips, pretzels, a box of crackers, and a large bag of popcorn next to the cooler. There was another bag with plates, cups, utensils, napkins, salt, and pepper.

I said, "Sophie, where are the place mats?" I was just kidding, but I wouldn't have been surprised if there were some in the car, somewhere. As it was, we could live for a week on what she had packed for a two-day trip.

Shortly after we had left the store, a heavy downpour started, slowing the cars on the road down to a crawl. While it made eating my sandwich a little easier, we weren't making very good time. It finally quit, thank goodness, and traffic began to move past the snail pace we had been doing for the past hour. We were once again heading for South Carolina for our first overnight stop.

Sophie was wound like a seven-day clock. It seemed with every mile we went, she chattered more. Ralph ignored her as best he could, and seemed to be just cruising along like he was alone in the front seat. I went in and out of dozing, just muttering an occasional yes or no to Sophie. Sophie finally broke through to Ralph with an urgent plea to stop at the next town that looked like it might

have a drugstore and gas station. She had a
headache, and she had to piddle. Ralph pulled off at
the next exit and, as we drove into the parking lot,
Sophie said that she hoped they had Goody
Powders.

I thought it was a candy bar, but when Sophie
got the packet, it sure didn't look like candy. Sophie
opened a Coke, ripped the packet open with her
teeth, then put her head back and poured this pow-
der on her tongue. She chased it down with half the
Coke and proclaimed that Goody still had the best
relief for headaches; she could feel hers lifting
already.

Everyone has his or her little quirks and odd
ways. Some you might call weird or strange (of
course, your own quirks count as perfectly normal
behavior), but one thing you never do is question
someone about these things. Unless, that is, you'd
been sitting in the car with him or her for the better
part of a day with nothing much to think about,
other than things like why on earth Ralph felt com-
pelled to get out three flannel towels every time we
stopped and completely wipe down the car. He also
washed the windshield at every stop, whether it
needed it or not. He'd done it about six times
already that day, and as I saw him begin his ritual
again, I couldn't hold back my curiosity any longer.
"Ralph, you have this car shining like a copper kettle."

"That's right. I intend to keep this Chevy looking just like this twenty years from now. We'll both be antiques, but the car, she'll look brand new."

We climbed back into the car and hit the road. We chatted now and then as the hours passed, and Sophie informed us about the major happenings she read about in the Virginia newspaper she had picked up at the drugstore.

Then I saw the sign saying we had crossed over into North Carolina. The radio was playing an oldie, "Once In A While," and we started to sing along. That kept my mind off my bladder for a little while, but I was starting to feel in desperate need of a pit stop. I had consumed more liquids than anyone should have in a confined space with no built-in facilities. I thought if I could just wait another hour, Sophie was sure to want out. Seems she was on a three-hour disposal schedule. I smiled to myself, feeling the excitement build. North Carolina! I unscrewed the top from a soda bottle and started to read my book.

Just then Sophie said, "Here comes a big one."

I put my book down, soda again between my knees, to look out the windshield, then out the side windows. What in hell was she talking about? All I saw were miles and miles of fields. Then I noticed that Sophie was taking off the jacket to her dress.

"Sophie, what are you talking about, here comes the big one?"

"Hot flash," she said. "Lasts a couple of minutes."

Ralph said, "Sophie, you don't get hot flashes anymore; those are power surges."

"Ralph, just shut your mouth and push that air conditioning on high," she snarled.

"Sophie, it's already on high."

"Then pass me an ice cube, would you?" I handed her over one wrapped in a paper towel, and she quieted down again.

I read several pages, than began to feel myself nodding off again. This was no easy feat, what with Sophie continually reading out loud from her gossip papers about something one of her favorite actors or actresses was up to.

Then I heard that noise, the dreaded "whoop, thump," that I heard not too long ago on the Parkway.

"What the hell was that?" Sophie said, pulling her nose out of the papers. "Why are we slowing down? Why are we pulling over? Why is the car going sideways?"

Ralph stopped the car and turned to her. He said, "Soph, what the hell do you think that sound was? It sounded like a tire going flat to me."

As I walked to the trunk I heard Ralph mutter, "Son of a bitch. The trunk is packed to the damn hinges, the tire is in the well, which means everything must come out."

I tried to help Ralph empty the trunk and place all the cases, bags, and gifts along the side of the road. He was sweating profusely, trying to loosen the uncooperative lugs that held the tire.

"At the factory, they put these sons of bitches on with power tools," he complained, grunting with effort. "How the hell do they expect someone to get them loose with this piece of shit tool they call a lug wrench?"

Sophie put her head out of the window and asked how he was doing. Ralph walked over to her open window with slow, deliberate steps. His face was red, the veins in his neck were pulsating, and he dripped sweat off his chin as he stuck his head in the window. He started to say something, thought better of it, and shook his head. I was thinking longingly of my Moose. He would have had the tire changed in a heartbeat. And made my heart beat a little faster while he was at it. Ah, well. We're a long way away from the Parkway.

The traffic just kept passing by, blowing exhaust and bad air. I could tell we had a big problem. Finally, a car pulled up behind Ralph and parked on the grass embankment. The door opened and a tall, lean fellow of about 30 came toward the car. He tucked his white undershirt into the waistband of his jeans as he approached.

"Do you folks need any help?" he asked.

"Yes, that would be appreciated," I replied.

While he was no Moose, I'd take him. This male angel of mercy went about setting up the jack and turning the lugs that were holding the deflated tire with little effort. His name was Alfred Skinner, he told Ralph as he twisted loose the lugs. His wife and two children were in the car. They were headed back to South Carolina to live with her parents on a farm. They should have never gone up North, he said, but they thought things would be better there. He removed the last lug with a grunt, wiped the sweat from his face, and told Ralph that he thought he could make more money up North—he was a carpenter, and a good one, he said—but it just didn't work out.

I glanced back at his car and saw his wife and two small children climb out. The kids clung to her side as she walked up to our Chevy. The boy looked to be about five, and the girl maybe eight, nine years old. They looked like a family who had seen some very hard times.

The children were dressed poorly, but they were clean. They weren't wearing any shoes, but that doesn't mean anything. No kid in his right mind would wear shoes if he had the chance to go barefoot, especially on a day like today. The boy was holding a baseball he told me he found. The girl was clutching a bald-headed, bare-assed doll that looked like it had seen better days.

As soon as Sophie spotted the children, she

jumped out of the car and swung into action.

"What's your name, honey?" she asked them. "How old are you all?" They were a little shy, but soon loosened up and began chatting with her. Then she said, "We have too many sandwiches for the three of us," and handed the wife and children each a sandwich and a cold soda, for which they smiled and thanked her. When she asked him, Alfred said he would have a drink and sandwich when he finished the tire.

That Sophie sure knew how to throw a roadside picnic. She pulled out paper plates and filled them with cheeses, pickles, and deviled eggs, plus a plate of chips. The wife said her name was Maggie, the son was Austin and their daughter was Jessica. The children made no response to their names; they were too busy eating. Dear, precious Sophie found a blanket that used to be in the trunk and now lay heaped on the side of the road with the rest of the trunk stuff. She shook it out and spread it on the grass, then sat there with the wife and children, talking to them like they were at a family reunion.

Several times I caught Ralph looking at these children and wondered what he was thinking. Alfred and Ralph repacked the trunk. While they were doing this, Ralph was telling them our destination was Macon, Georgia, for their niece's wedding.

Sophie then made a plate of food for Alfred and

a cold soda. No one refused the offer of the food and drinks. Ralph enjoyed telling them I had never been further south than New Jersey. Alfred said that he knew I would like South Carolina, and I would really like the area where the wedding would be held. "Virgin country," Ralph described it. "No big city, no parkways, no department stores for shopping," he paused and gave Sophie a look. "Where we are going can best be described as just big, open, beautiful country."

"Amen," said Alfred, adding that he was looking forward to getting back home again.

Everyone finished eating, and we repacked the trunk as Ralph thanked Alfred one last time. As Ralph extended his hand, I saw a ten dollar bill pass to Alfred.

"Thanks again, fellow," he said. As cantankerous as Ralph could become when things went wrong, he got over it just as quickly. As he got into the car, he laughed, and then started singing "On the Road Again."

We headed south again, and, after what seemed like eternity, we saw a sign for gas and food. We knew they had rest rooms, which we were all more than eager for. That last soda I had while we were waiting for Alfred to fix the tire was one too many for me.

This was a combination of gas station with one pump and old-fashioned country store. When I asked where the rest rooms were, the man at the register pointed his finger outside. I went in the direction he pointed, and there it stood: a rough wooden closet sitting on bricks. Inside was a chamber of horrors: The seat was cut out of a piece of rough-looking board, and you wouldn't believe the smell that emanated from it. I made quick work of it, let me tell you. The air in the parking lot, even with the fumes from idling cars, sure smelled sweet.

There was a large, black, cast-iron pot on the porch with a sign labeled "hot boiled peanuts" made from a lid of a beer carton, and small, brown bags lying next to the kettle marked "twenty five cents. Help yourself. Pay inside." I bypassed that one, having already tasted that particular delicacy. Inside the store was a variety of goods. There was a basket on the counter that was full of eggs; there were stacks of bread, and loads of small boxes holding onions, sweet potatoes, apples, and tomatoes.

"So, you're headed to South Carolina," drawled the man at the register. "I overheard you talking to my friend, the man outside cleaning his windshield," he said in answer to my puzzled look.

"Do you know how much further we have to go?" I asked."Oh, it's not very far. Just down yonder a piece."

"How far would you say that 'down yonder' might be? In miles, that is."

He scratched the few wispy hairs on the top of

his small head and said, "I reckon about two more hours."

"I reckon that two more hours could be about another hundred miles."

He scratched another small area behind his ear, and then took out a penknife from his overalls pocket. He picked up one of the apples, cut out a slice and put it in his mouth. He chewed a bit, looked as thoughtful as a cow chewing its cud, and said, "Well maybe," and put another piece of apple in his mouth.

"Maybe what?"

"Maybe more, maybe less. Depends on how fast you drive."

Sophie pushed me aside and sidled up to the counter. She handed the man a dollar. "Wait till you try these," she said, opening a bag that read fried pork rinds in big, red letters.

I looked at the bag and shuddered. "Not in this lifetime."

The aggravating man rang up the pork rinds on his twelve keyed register and handed Sophie her change. He cut another wedge from the apple, and, chewing, said, "You know, they ruined those pork rinds when they fancied them with barbecue taste. The regular fried rinds with a bottle of grape soda go real good." He gestured with the knife at the counter. "We have some hard-boiled eggs in vinegar—ten cents apiece—and the pigs feet in vinegar were made yesterday." I grabbed Sophie and pulled her out the door before she bought some. The rinds were bad enough.

Back on the road again, squashed into the back seat. The bag of chips kept falling on my head, and I just couldn't get comfortable.

"Sophie had you and Ralph driven down with Sam's parents, where would you put all this stuff?" I asked, shoving the bag back behind the cooler.

He laughed. "That's easy. We would have hooked up a trailer to their new Cadillac."

"Ralph, there are times you are not funny as you think they are," Sophie said, giving Ralph a poke with her elbow. "Sam's parents had a van they used to take on trips. If they still had it, we would have used that driving down. But I guess they must have gotten rid of it somewhere down the line. What do you think, Ralph? I haven't been by their house in ages, but didn't you go see them when you were up visiting old friends in Bayonne a while back?"

"They weren't home, but I didn't see it in the driveway," Ralph said, looking puzzled. "Now that you mention it, seems strange that we haven't seen your only brother in so long."

"That's not for a lack of trying," Sophie replied. "They never invite us over, and when we call them to come for dinner or a picnic, they say they have other plans. Remember, I invited them for Christmas last year, but they had other plans." She sighed. "That's probably just as well. Sam would not have come if they were there."

My ears pricked up at this. "Why wouldn't Sam want to spend Christmas with her parents?" I piped up from the backseat.

Sophie looked at Ralph, who just stared out the windshield at the passing scenery. "You know, honey, we thought about that, too. I mean, and no disrespect intended, her mother is a bit of a bitch, but I could put up with her. But anytime we've tried to get them all together, Sam just turns white as a ghost. We were so happy to have Sam come for the holidays last year. It just didn't seem worth it to ask questions and upset her."

Despite all the stops, we were making pretty good time. The summer vacation traffic wasn't as heavy as Ralph had anticipated.

"Hey, Sophie," he said. "Remember that time we went on vacation to Maine?"

"Sure do. We got lost. And you had the nerve to say, 'We may be lost, but at least we are making good time.' We only got lost because this man," she whacked his shoulder lightly, "this macho man will not stop and ask directions. So we drove four hours in the wrong direction before you'd finally stop at a gas station and get pointed in the right direction. Then it was four more hours getting back to the way we should have been going in the first place."

As we shared a laugh, the sky was turning from

blue to a midnight black. Sophie said, "Dear God, I hope it doesn't thunder and lightning. I am deathly afraid of storms." With that, a crack of thunder seemed to roll right across the highway. The rain was heavy, making it almost impossible to see even with the wipers rotating back and forth to their full capacity. Ralph was trying to make light of it, but I could tell he was having a difficult time trying to see the road. "Girls, this is what is known down here as a Southern spritz," he joked, trying to lighten Sophie's mood. She wasn't paying attention, though. Her knuckles were white where she gripped the dashboard, and she flinched at each resounding blast.

As for me, this "Southern spritz" looked more like a Northern monsoon. I personally could not conceive how Ralph or any other driver could see beyond the hood of the car. We pulled over under an overpass, along with a couple of other cars whose drivers decided they didn't need to try and prove they were superior to Mother Nature.

A few people got out of their cars to take a welcome stretch. Much as I like Sophie and Ralph, it was nice to speak to someone else for a change. Sophie, being miss chatty Cathy, enjoyed it even more. Now that we were stopped, I could see that Ralph was a bit shaken. He went into the glove compartment and took out a case that holds three cigars, lit one, and just sat there for a few minutes. After a few puffs, he looked over at me and smiled. Then a kid got out of one of the other cars with a cap pistol, holding a roll of caps that he intended to detonate while he was granted his freedom from the captivity of the backseat.

"I would like to shove that gun and the roll of caps up that kid's ass," Ralph growled.

"Come on, Ralph," I chided. "You were a kid once, too."

"I was never a kid. I was born, went to school, and went to work in a feed store when I was 12. That was heavy work. On weekends, I would cut and sell wood with my old man for the extra money. There were eight of us in three bedrooms. I still can't figure out how Mom came home with one chicken and fed all of us a dinner. We ate a lot of potatoes, bread with jelly, and bologna sandwiches, I know that. I got my high school diploma when I was twenty two years old by going to school nights. Then I got older. I was never a kid." He looked at his cigar, took another puff and threw it into the road, where it sizzled, then went out. The rain had let up to a fine drizzle.

"Let's get going," Ralph said.

As we were pulling out, Sophie said, "There are so many nice people you meet when traveling. The older couple were going to Florida to see their new grandson. I was thinking when Sam has a baby; we will be the great aunt and uncle. Won't that be wonderful? The younger couple with the boy was going home."

"You mean that obnoxious midget with the cap pistol?" Ralph snorted. "They probably took him out of reform school for the summer." He looked in the rear view mirror and winked at me.

I was thinking Sam would probably be a good mother. When you chip away her shell, her "I don't give a damn" attitude, when you finally get under her skin, you see the warm, caring woman underneath. She just wants and needs love and, most of all trust. Maybe Harry was the one who can make that happen. I had not seen her for almost two weeks, and it seemed like years. In just two more days, I'd see her walk down the aisle. At least, I hoped I would.

Finally, I spotted the sign welcoming us to South Carolina. I looked around, but it didn't look much different from North Carolina to me. Everything was still flat as a board. I looked off into the distance, and saw a cloud of smoke rising from one of the fields.

"Hey, you two up front! Look over there—all those fields are on fire!"

Ralph just laughed, "Down here, when the crops are harvested, the farmers set fires to burn the fields before putting in the new plantings. It puts something back in the soil."

Sophie didn't appear to have heard this last exchange. As usual, she seemed to be absorbed with thinking about her stomach. "When we pass through a town, stop at Piggly Wiggly. I want to get some things I haven't had in years: some Moon Pies."

Now she had my attention. "What is a Piggly Wiggly and what are Moon Pies?".

Ralph said, "Piggly Wiggly is a food store, and Moon Pies are a small snack cake that Sophie does not need. But I will stop, since she asked so nicely." Just then the car seemed to hesitate. I noticed that happening a few times over the last couple of hours, but hadn't thought too much of it. Ralph had noticed also, but he said it wasn't serious. Probably just some dirt in the gas line or maybe a few wires got wet from all the water on the road. "It will work its way out," Ralph assured me. "No reason to be concerned." But I was, so Ralph said he would pull over and check under the hood. We took the next exit and started cruising through the small town just off the highway. Ralph found a turnout on the road, and pulled over. Just then, we saw flashing lights behind us. Ralph got out and met the patrolman halfway. He was with the officer for a few minutes, and then he opened the trunk. Ralph slammed the trunk closed and came back to the car.

Sophie was straining at the bit to hear the news. "He knows I hate it when he makes me wait to hear what happened."

Ralph laughed. "The officer asked me why I pulled over, if I had a problem. I told him we pulled over because it was time for you to nurse the baby. I invited him to come up front and check, but he turned red as a beet and declined. Did you see him almost run back to the patrol car?" Ralph began to laugh like hell, and I joined him.

Sophie said, "Damn you. What if he checked?" Ralph, still laughing, said, "Soph, even cops are respectful of a woman nursing her pup. I knew he wouldn't look inside the car. Damn, that was funny." He hit the steering wheel, laughing so hard he began to wheeze.

Sophie was still pretty steamed. She opened her bag of fried pork rinds. I gave her a soda from the chest, and that seemed to cool her down.

We drove on for a few minutes in a silence that was complete except for the sounds of Sophie crunching those pork rinds.

Then, still fuming, Sophie said, "Why in the world did you have to open the trunk?"

"I showed him all the gifts you were taking for the wedding. I would've shown him the backseat full of gifts too, except I couldn't." He began to snigger again. "Because you were nursing the baby."

We were saved when Sophie saw the Piggly Wiggly store. We pulled into the lot, which was very busy with working people stopping to get lunch fixings.

I went on a tour of the store, looking at many new and different items, and had a cup of coffee. Sophie was nowhere to be found. This was nothing new or unusual; by now I had figured out that she had an almost physical need to walk through every store she could along the way and buy something. I was really enjoying just being able to stretch my legs. The manager came over and asked me in a sweet Southern accent if he could help me to find something. I thanked him and thought, wasn't that nice. Where I come from, they seldom help you, even when you ask. The Piggly Wiggly sold a lot more than groceries: I saw beer, wine, fishing bait, fishing poles, and firewood in six-log bundles. The best part was that I saw that part of the service included having someone bag your purchases, push the cart to your car, and put your bags in the trunk for you. They wouldn't even accept a tip.

Sophie finally appeared. After checking out her groceries, she handed me a Moon Pie. Wait until you try this," she said. I told her I would keep it for later.

After what seemed like never-ending miles of driving in spite of all the stops we made, our driver and tour guide announced that within a couple of hours we would arrive in Charleston.

"Now if you will look to the right and left of the highway," Ralph intoned, "You will see wooden structures with just tar pad on top to keep out the heat of the sun." I looked where he pointed, and sure enough, there were all shapes and sizes of baskets hanging on hooks from wooden slab boards. It looked like the baskets were made by hand from sweet grass by the women sitting on stools at the huts.

"You want to stop and buy a basket?" asked Ralph, already pulling over. "Why not? Who knows when you will get down here again?" As we pulled over to the huts, I saw that they were pretty flimsy looking; it seemed a strong wind could blow them apart. The black girls sitting outside looked to be about late teens or perhaps just a few years older. There were three small children on blankets playing with what looked like oyster shells. Then I saw a black woman who looked like she'd endured many years of a hard life, never knowing what easy times were about. She was busy making her basket and never looked up at us, though she did say a few words to the children. I imagined she was their grandmother. The baskets were beautiful, and we bought four of them. Of course, they ended up in the backseat with me.

Chapter 23

We arrived in Charleston at about eight that night. We checked in at a bed and breakfast home that looked like the grand house Tara in Gone with the Wind. Oh, I was about to have my first genuine air-cooled experience; all rooms had ceiling fans. I was taken to a bedroom with a four-poster canopy bed; the wash stand in the room reflected the dignity of many past years. All was awesome beyond words. Real lace curtains hung from long, wide windows with shutters. I looked out at a wrought-iron fence that surrounded the vast well-manicured grounds. Just then a horse and carriage passed by, its driver wearing a high black hat, black coat with tails, and shiny boots.

It was hard to believe that this was real, not a dream or a movie set. I decided a ride in that carriage would be something I would have to take some time. I fell in love with this place called Charleston then and there, and just that one brief glimpse of it would stay within my memory until someday I would be able to return. But right then, I was so very tired. I curled up in that huge bed and snuggled down into a well of luxury.

Ralph wanted to leave as early as possible the next morning, which meant I wouldn't get a chance to get out and look around Charleston. It also meant I would have to forget that carriage ride. Oh well. I promised myself that I would come back someday and get to know this enchanted city. I opened my door with my small overnight case in hand, and bumped into a young black girl steering a vacuum into Sophie and Ralph's room, which happened to be next to mine.

"Good morning ma'am," she said politely. "Your friends are in the dining room. It's down the stairs, turn right, second room."

I found Sophie and Ralph in the dining room surrounded by fellow guests. They were telling Sophie and Ralph something about the history of Charleston. I am certain one of the owners of the bread and breakfast told them there were over a hundred and eighty churches in the area.

We were on the road by eight, next stop: Macon, wherever that was. As we drove through the streets, I admired all the handsome mansions surrounded by vast gardens that looked like every inch of grass was manicured. Huge old magnolia bushes arched over many a yard and I saw many bushes and trees that were not at all familiar to me. Ralph said that the beautiful lavender-blooming trees I saw were called crepe myrtles. He also told me, showing off what he had learned at breakfast, that the

Charleston Museum, which was founded in seventeen seventy three was the oldest museum in the
United States. Trees and gardens appeared to sur-
round the entire Charleston area. Cobblestone
streets reflected the sounds of horses' hooves
pulling fine carriages to their destinations.

As Charleston faded into the distance, I looked
for other ways to amuse myself. Looking into the
passing cars was interesting, at least for a while.
Seems like everyone was eating or drinking something as they were heading for another day at work.
I decided to clean out my purse, which Ralph said
looked like a flight bag.

Ralph glanced in the mirror and saw what I was
doing. "I wish Sophie would do that once in a
while. But forget the purse; her closets are what she
needs to clean out. You wouldn't believe what she's
got in there. Lots of clothes she will never wear
again, like dozens of pairs of shoes that she hasn't
worn since Truman was in office. Not to mention
her tap-dancing shoes from when she was nine."

"What?" Sophie said. "Don't start on my closets. They are none of your concern."

But Ralph wasn't finished yet. "Do you know
that half the dresses hanging on the racks still have
tags on them? Know why she's never worn them,
because they damn well don't fit, and they are never
going to fit. You see, Sophie cannot pass up bar-
gains, even for things she can't use. If it's on sale for
half price, Sophie buys it."

"That's not true, and besides, Ralph, you don't know what the hell you're talking about. Styles change."

"So did your body, Sophie," Ralph rejoined. I decided it was time to change the subject before things really got out of control. Besides, there was something that had been worrying me ever since we started on this odyssey to Georgia.

"Listen, you two. I have been thinking. We all know how unpredictable Sam can be. I mean, she'll just go ahead and change her mind about anything she feels like changing her mind about. She'll plan one thing, then turn around and do something totally crazy just because it's fun or because it will shock everyone."

"I suppose so, but what's your point?" Sophie said.

"I'll tell you what the point is. I'm worried. What if she ditches Harry before the wedding? I mean, anything could have happened in the last couple of days since we've talked with her. Suppose they got married in some small church or at a justice of the peace on the way down? Sam has no idea I am coming for the wedding. I know she'll come through with the reception. She doesn't want to disappoint her grandparents. But I wouldn't put it past her to talk Harry into saying their wedding vows somewhere else, just to screw up her parents. That would be an all-time high for Sam."

Ralph looked at Sophie. "Do you think she would do something like that?"

It took what seemed like forever for Sophie to answer. She finally put her head back and said, "I have no idea what Sam has been thinking for a long time now. I was surprised, very surprised, when she called me and told me she was marrying Harry. I mean, she's been engaged who-can-remember-how-many-times before, but there was something different in her voice this time. When she asked me what I thought about her decision, I could only tell her that if she loves him and she feels he would make her happy, it would make me happy. But it's hard to take it seriously. There have been too many times when Sam said she was going to settle down, and then she'd back out of it. She would say, 'I think this is it, Sophie. I think I would like some children, too.' Like she was ordering life from a menu."

"We have to just remember that Sam will do what she thinks is best for her," said Ralph. "We should quit being judgmental and just wait and see what's what when we get there. We will know then what she wants. She knows that we love her, and whatever she ends up doing, we will understand and treat her decision with respect." Sometimes, Ralph could be a very wise man.

Just then the car hesitated again.

"Don't worry. I figured out what that is," Ralph said. "It comes from using different gas each time we fill up. Air gets into the engine, and then passes the gas. That's a good one: it passes the gas," he said, chuckling. Sophie, who once again had picked up her movie magazines, just harrumphed.

"You know, Sophie, all those actor guys you're always reading about in them movie magazines are all gay," he said to needle her. The only real man out there is John Wayne. I'm here to tell you that is one honest fact."

I started to rummage through my purse again. The board of health would have condemned what was lying in the dark hole of that bag: a half-eaten Mounds bar, a bag wrapped with an elastic band holding crumbs of potato chips, loose Chiclets, a toothbrush, deodorant, and a whistle. And oh, my God. I don't believe this. There lying in the midst of the clutter was a wrapped, lavender, luminous condom.

Sophie said, "What's wrong?"

"Well, Christmas three years ago one of my funny male friends from the office gave me half of a nightgown, you know to the waist, from that California nightwear store. It had a lavender bow, and this was tied to it, along with a card that read, 'This way you'll know where it's at in the dark.'" I held up the condom, and Ralph just about lost it.

"Let me see that," he yelled, grabbing at the condom over the backrest of the seat. "If you don't want it, I'll take it and have some fun with that."

"Ralph, honey, look at me," Sophie said. "I think you are running a quart low."

"Sophie, I only want to show it to my card-playing cronies. They will think I am a real swinger." Sophie opened the window, and out went the lavender, luminous condom onto the green grass of the highway.

Sophie put down her magazine.

"I have been meaning to ask, did your Aunt Annie ever come down for the weekend?"

"No, she called and canceled. Seems she heard that a large estate somewhere in Wilkes-Barre was having a sale. It was owned by a wealthy mine owner who passed away at age ninety. He outlived his heirs and was having everything auctioned off, which meant a house full of antiques. She was headed up there with her truck."

I told Sophie all about her date with J.C., the undertaker who had the hots for my aunt. They did go to dinner at the new inn, and when they were seated, he took the chair next to her rather than sit across the table. She thought that was because he wore a hearing aid. Then during their conversation he would put his hand on her knee. She straight out let him know the only dessert he was getting would be from the menu.

"Why do they call him J.C.?" Sophie asked.

"It seemed a lot easier than Jeremiah Coffin," I told her.

Ralph laughed. "That is one hell of a name for a

guy in his business. I remember as a kid that they always had the corpse viewing in the house. They would come in, put the wooden v-shaped platform down with boards across, then the red velvet drop cloth with fringes over that and set the casket on top. They even embalmed them at the house. One of the families would sit up with them all night, I guess so they wouldn't feel alone. All us kids sure liked funerals and weddings: plenty of food, pies, and cakes.

"My brother and I were big for our age," Ralph continued. "He was fifteen and I was thirteen when this guy Sully died. He owned the corner bar, but they thought it would be tacky to lay him out there, so they put him in his living room.

"Now Sully was just a runt, meaning small and skinny, and he never married—who the hell would want him? When the undertaker called his sister in Bayonne and told her Sully had passed away, she just said "Good," and hung up. My brother and two of our buddies decided to go into the house around midnight, take Sully out of his coffin and sit him in the front seat of his car. We put his hands on the steering wheel, we covered his head with his cap— he always wore a cap because he had a pointy head, smooth and hairless as a baby's ass.

"The next morning our old man came into the bedroom we shared with another brother, and shook us awake. He said something very strange happened during the night. When the preacher and undertaker came to the house that morning to check Sully for the services, he was gone. They found him in the front seat of his roadster. They had to put him back in the coffin where he belonged. 'I don't suppose you fellows know anything about it?' he said.

We swore that, "no, of course, we didn't know anything about anything. We were in bed early." Old man broke out into a fit of laughter, and, of course, we joined him.

"Ralph, did you really do that awful thing?"

"Sophie, like we told our Pop, we were in bed early." And the miles spun on under our wheels. I could smell Georgia in the air. Or maybe that was just the peach cobbler; Sophie had just pulled out of the cooler.

Chapter 24

What was that noise? I slowly opened my eyes and looked around. It was very late, and very dark, when we pulled into the motel last night. Where was I? What day was it? After two days on the road with Sophie and Ralph, I was all confused. I rubbed my eyes and looked blearily around the room. Next to the bed was a floor lamp standing very tall and erect, with a long-tasseled shade. Standing beside a big, overstuffed chair was an old-fashioned chest of drawers. On top of the dresser was a glass pitcher and two colored glasses on a white doily; on the small wall over the small dresser was a small mirror hanging on the wall.

There, that noise again, like something scratching. There was a nightstand, the bed, and I, and none of us seemed to be feeling particularly itchy. Maybe rats? Or maybe even something worse? Who knew what kinds of animals were there in the South? It could be a giant cockroach for all I knew.

I stood up on the bed, afraid to put my feet on the floor, and was momentarily distracted by the view out the window. Now this was country. No cars passing by, just quiet like another world.

There it was again. I cocked my head, listening.

It was the door, something was scratching outside the door. I found my robe and slippers, thinking that should this thing chase me, going into the motel office screaming for help in a short nightie was no way to start the day.

Slowly, I opened the door, expecting a hound from hell at the very least. Instead, I was greeted by a large Collie, who promptly sat down and put her paw out for me to shake.

"Well, where did you come from?" I asked, like she was ready for a conversation. Of course, she must live here. It was very late when we checked in after unloading the car of what we thought was enough to get us comfortable to sleep. I hardly knew what the surroundings were and I could care less who else occupied these grounds. We certainly did not take a resident count.

She pushed the door open with her long nose, padded over to the bed and jumped up, then just sat there looking at me. I gave her a few pats, than heard a tap on the door. When I opened it, I found a woman standing there with a small tray covered with white paper napkins.

"Thought you might like a cup of coffee," she said. "I understand you take it black. I see you met Missy. She has a nose for trouble, likes to check out units to see how much attention she can get. My name is Margaret," she said, holding the tray out for me. "My husband and I own this motel and gas station.

"You have a beautiful dog. She seems to enjoy meeting people."

"I was painting the outside wood frames on my window boxes and she came out of those woods back there. That was about three months ago, and she has been here ever since. I took her to a vet in town, and he checked her out real good. She was fine, wasn't wearing any kind of a tag, just kina thin. Reckon all she needed was a couple of good meals. I left word with the vet and a sign in town with her description and our phone number. Like I mentioned, anyone who lost her should come here, but no one has claimed her. My husband and I took a real good liking to her." She gave Missy a pat. "We got to call her Missy, after she spent a few days with us because she made certain she never missed a meal."

"Come over to our house for breakfast. Our place is just behind the station. My husband tells everyone I lay out a nice spread. Ralph and Sophie have eaten already. Missy will show you the way when you're ready."

That they had already eaten did not surprise me. After all, it was all of eight o'clock. By my watch, those two would soon be thinking about lunch. Missy lay on the bed with her head on her front paws; watched me dress in a pair of shorts, sneakers, and a tank top. It was too early to put on my wedding outfit. I sipped some of the excellent coffee Margaret had left me on the dresser, and then felt an urge to explore.

"Come on, Missy, let's go outside and see where I slept last night," I said. She leapt off the bed and followed me out the door, her toenails clicking against the hardwood floor. Outside it was just country quiet. I looked up and down the dirt road by the motel, but didn't see anything coming or going either way. Either the road was closed, or we really did land in the backside of nowhere.

About twenty feet from the motel was a small gas station with two pumps. Missy led me around the back, where I found a white frame house. The smells coming from the screen door were incredible. As we went up the steps, I felt like I was getting a clue about how Sam's mornings had been down on Memaw and Pepaw's farm.

I knocked hesitantly on the screen door, then Missy pushed it open for me with her nose, and I followed her inside. What a wonderful old-fashioned kitchen! The heavy wooden table would easily seat eight; nearby were a woodstove and a regular stove with an oven. There was a rocker at one window. On the sill lay a small bag with a pull string of tobacco, a couple packs of cigarette papers and box matches, a long single sofa against one wall, and an antique clock that looked like it had ticked away many years on the wall above the sofa. A small room next to the kitchen was storage for all her canning on rows and rows of shelves. A large basket of sweet potatoes, bags of pecans were hanging from hooks. What looked like a white burlap bag of flour, a large basket filled with apples, and another basket with peaches. I then heard her call that breakfast was on the table.

Margaret looked up from her work at the countertop, wiped her hands on her apron, and with a cheery smile said, "We have home-fried potatoes, eggs, ham, bacon, hot biscuits, grits, homemade peach preserves, and cereal. What's your pleasure?"

I chose the cereal, with a warm biscuit and some peach preserves. She was stirring the fried potatoes and thick slices of ham in a huge cast-iron pan on the woodstove. Margaret's other half, Skipper, came in, took one look at my plate, and said, "You city gals eat like birds."

He informed me that Sophie and Ralph had gotten up at six, ate at six-thirty, and knew all there was to know about this area by seven-thirty.

Missy, who had settled herself down by my chair, gave a small growl as four fellows walked into the kitchen. Seems they were staying at the motel, doing some road work in Macon. One of the men ordered country ham and eggs over easy. I looked at his plate when Margaret set it down in front of him. There was this mealy looking white stuff spilling over the yellows of his eggs. When I asked him what that was, he said it was grits, and you mix it up with your eggs. No thank you. The ham looked good, though, so I asked Margaret for a slice. Well, I put a piece of ham in my mouth, and the more I chewed, the saltier it became. I thought to myself, what kind of ham is this? I felt like I was licking a salt stick.

Everyone was exchanging stories, which suited me fine. I was enjoying my biscuit with preserves, just listening. When the conversation fell into a lull, I said, "Margaret, I sure wish I could get these preserves up home. Delicious. Where do you get your peaches?" Fourteen eyes, including Missy's, stared at me like I had just asked a room full of Baptists to attend a Catholic mass.

Margaret broke the silence, "Girl, where do you get the finest peaches grown in any state? Right here, of course. Why, haven't your people up North heard of Georgia peaches? There are no peaches like a Georgia peach, no place has pecans like Georgia." She was peeling apples to make pies for lunch, but you can be sure I was not about to ask where she got those.

It was still four hours before we had to get dressed for the wedding. I located Sophie and Ralph and told them I was taking a walk around before I got ready. When we were leaving the house, Margaret put her hand on my shoulder and said, "When you folks get back later, stop by. The pies will be ready, and I'll have some fresh coffee

brewing." I dropped a couple dollars into the dona-
tion basket on the end table as I left.

Missy walked with me down the road, keeping
the Shady Maple Motel in sight. I sat down on a
large tree stump, and Missy joined me. "This is
really country," I murmured to Missy. "Nothing in
sight either way." It was great having a dog for company. I could tell her everything, and not only would
she listen, but I could be assured that she would
never repeat it.

"So, Missy, what do you think?" I scratched her
ears lightly, and she began to pant. "Will Sam actually go through with it this time, or was this trip all
for nothing? You know, it wouldn't be the first time
she left some poor guy standing at the altar. But it
would be the farthest she ever made him go to get
humiliated like that." Missy didn't answer me, but
she did rest her head on my knee. "You're right," I
said. "Guess I'll just have to wait and see. I sure
wish I could see Sam this morning, though. That
would put my mind at ease."

Missy stood up and gave a small woofing
sound. Looking up the road, I saw some dust flying.
Then a car came into view. They stopped and asked
me if there was a gas station nearby, and a place to
get breakfast. I pointed to the motel. They thanked
me and drove on. It was about time to head back
and get ready for Sam's big day.

The walls must have been made of fiberboard,
or whatever else comes even thinner than that. As I

was showering, I could hear Ralph was on the other side of the partition, singing loud. I heard him drop the soap in the stall, say, "Damn it," and then pick up volume again on a rousing rendition of "Nothing Could Be Finer than to be in Carolina in the Morning." I felt like knocking on the wall and telling him not to quit his day job.

I slipped into a pink chiffon dress with rose-colored shoes and bag. No gloves. Finally, I was finished, and if I did say so myself, I thought I looked pretty damn good for the occasion. I stepped outside and there was Ralph, all spit-polished with a rose in his buttonhole.

Sophie emerged just as Ralph completed a long whistle in my direction. Ralph said, "You know, Sophie, you look just as beautiful as the day we were married. He leaned over and kissed her on the cheek, then put his arm around her. "Can you believe, sweetheart, that I can still fit into my suits from twenty years ago? They don't make them like that anymore."

"You got that right, honey," she said, looking at me. "When I met Ralph, he didn't own a suit. The first one he bought was for our wedding, which just so happens to be the one you are looking at right now. Five years after we were married I bought him a suit for Christmas. Last Christmas, I bought him another suit: a nice, gray, double-breasted one. So what does he wear today? His very first suit from our wedding."

Ralph said, "While you girls were sleeping, I washed the car so you two lovely ladies can ride to the church in a clean chariot. I did have a problem starting it, though. When we leave tomorrow, I'll stop at a station on the way back where they have a mechanic to check her out, but I'm still sure it's nothing."

"Ralph, what on earth do you have in that big shopping bag?" Sophie inquired, noting a giant sack bulging on the ground by the trunk.

Ralph just laughed. "It's a surprise, girls."

We decided to come back to the motel to change after the wedding. We had nearly two hours to kill before the reception would start, and you couldn't have much fun in outfits like these. Besides, we decided we wouldn't mind having a piece of that apple pie and coffee before starting out again. We all climbed into the car, and Ralph looked in the rearview mirror. "Have to put a couple of pounds on that girl back there. We are the beautiful people, going to see a beautiful girl we all love so much marry a guy that better make her happy, or he'll have us to answer to. Now let's hit the road."

A plume of dust bloomed behind the car as we headed down the road toward where Margaret had told us the church would be. When we pulled up in front of the small white church, I couldn't help but think it would make a great Christmas card. Its white steeple pointed up into a cloudless blue sky, and the lawn surrounding it was a deep, rich green. There were several cars parked on the grass in front, and a good crowd of people was standing around talking. Some children were running around playing some kind of rowdy game. Every now and then, a parent would interrupt their conversation to threaten a kid to cut it out before they soiled their best outfits. The children could have been deaf for all the good that did.

Now Sam hadn't lived here since she was seventeen. Surely not all these people were here for the wedding? Eavesdropping on the conversation around me, I soon figured out that anything at all out of the ordinary is a cause for celebration in a small country like this. Some were curious to see the bride and groom. Others were there for the funeral that was to take place later. A car pulled up with four young people just out for a ride. When they found out there was a wedding happening, they parked the car and strolled over to join the crowd. We walked over to wait by the steps for the bride and groom. I could feel my anxiety growing. Oh please, Sam, I thought to myself, please do the right thing and show up. A few of the folks nearby started up a conversation, which was good. It helped distract me from my doubts. Ralph let it be known that we came all the way from New Jersey for the wedding.

We ran into a thin-faced, sharp-nosed man dressed in a black robe. "We're Sam's aunt and uncle," Ralph said proudly. The man turned out to be Harry Harper, the one who'd be officiating at a triple crown of a day: a wedding, a funeral, and a bingo game.

"You sure are a busy man," Ralph said to him.

"You don't know the half of it," the preacher said in funereal tones. He seemed a little dour to be doing a wedding, but I guessed that, in a town this small, you took what you could get.

Ralph told the preacher he was going to be the best man for Harry. And yes, he had the rings, Ralph said, patting his coat pocket.

The pastor said, "It's a shame Harry doesn't have any family coming for the wedding, the poor man being an orphan and all. At least Sam has her mother to stand for her as her matron of honor."

Ralph gave me a poke and said, "She was going to ask you to be her maid of honor, but you said you couldn't come. She sure is going to be some kind of surprised, now, won't she?"

I nodded. "A good surprise, I hope. I wonder where she is, anyway." I glanced around, but didn't see anyone bride-like hanging about. It was getting very warm, and I was dying of thirst. Someone standing in the doorway of the church took pity on me and mentioned that there was some sweet tea inside. Ralph went into the church, and handed me one of the two plastic cups he returned with. He said he would share his with Sophie, but she didn't want any.

"I'll have to pee enough already from all that breakfast coffee," she said. Ralph took a swallow and made a sour face.

"Damn, that tastes just like yours, Soph."

Sophie just shook her head and started to walk away. "Sophie, honey, wait for me," he said, going after her.

Just then I saw a big, shiny Cadillac pull up, streaked with road dust. I squinted in the bright sun to make out the inhabitants, but I didn't realize it was the wedding party until I saw Sam's father emerge from the driver's side and help her mother out of the car. Then Harry got out and held out his hand to Sam, who somehow made getting out of the car look like a grand entrance to the Academy Awards. She looked absolutely radiant. The dress we worked so hard to find turned out to be well worth the effort: it looked like it was made just for her. Something in my heart loosened up a little when I saw her. Everything was going to be okay, I just knew it.

As Sam started picking her way over the lawn toward the steps, she looked up and saw me. She let out a great whoop of joy and positively flew across the grass.

"What a wonderful surprise," she said. "I wanted so much for you to come."

I gave her a big hug, being careful not to mess up her hair. "You have never looked happier or more beautiful."

She then threw her arms around Sophie and Ralph. "Now that we're all here, let's let the wedding begin."

Harry was not far behind her. He grabbed Ralph's hand and gave it a hard shake, then did the same to Sophie. He started to hold out his hand to me, but I swatted it away and gave him a big hug. I think the man was a little dazed. But boy, did he look good. He was wearing a tan suit, a dark brown shirt, a tan-and-rust tie, and dark brown loafers. His hair, which he usually wore below the ears, was professionally styled; even his nails were clean. I said, "Harry, you clean up real good."

He smiled and hugged me back. "I want to thank you for introducing me to Sam. Your next oil change is on me."

As we entered the church, I spotted a box of bamboo fans on a table near the door. Before I could ask what that was about, Sophie handed one to me. As I walked further into the church, I noticed that all the women were holding fans. Guess the church wasn't air-cooled. I could feel the heat building already from all the people who were gathering inside. Ralph said he had to go see a man about a horse, and he'd be back in a minute.

There was no apparent seating arrangement. However, Sophie and I did get two seats together at the end of the third row. Then the minister came down the aisle and took his place at the altar. He looked much more somber than he had out in the daylight. I nudged Sophie and whispered, "He looks more like an undertaker than a preacher, doesn't he?"

She nodded, fanning herself, and said, "Maybe we should introduce him to your Aunt Annie."

Ralph came down the aisle and took his place on the altar next to Harry. The preacher began by making an announcement. He cleared his throat and said, "Reverend Huggins will not be able to preside over the wedding as he got laid, uh-hem, which is laid up, with a severe attack of gout. I, however, will perform the wedding ceremony." He cleared his throat again, and then said, "Let us begin." He waved to the piano player, who bent over the keyboard and began to play "Here Comes the Bride." Come on, Sam, I thought. The music played for several bars before I finally saw the bride come through the open door.

She strode down the aisle carrying a bouquet of yellow roses, looking for all the world like an angel transformed into human form by the magic of love. Her mother trailed along behind her, looking her usual regal best. But where was her father? I scanned the congregation until I finally spotted him over in the first row.

Harry, who had been pulling nervously at his collar until I was afraid he was going to choke himself, let his hand drop to his side as he gazed, mesmerized, at the vision of Sam mounting the steps to the altar. When she reached his side, she took his elbow and a gave it a little squeeze. Her mother gave her a kiss, and then was joined by her father, who gave her a peck on the cheek, then took her hand and ceremoniously placed it in Harry's palm. Both parents turned and went back to the front pew without a backward glance.

"Dearly beloved, we are gathered together here today to join..." the preacher intoned, but I was distracted by a "rat ta ta" sound. "Sophie, what was that?" I whispered.

"Somebody let go a fart," she whispered back. "Best start fanning yourself now." The smell was starting to drift our way. Dear God, it was awful. Smelled like something died inside of whoever let that one go. I could tell the progression of the fart odor by watching the fans, which sped up as it wafted by. Sophie and I had ours going fast as hummingbird wings, let me tell you. I just hoped it wouldn't make it up on the altar. Poor Sam would burst out laughing, I just knew it.

"Do you, Samantha, take Harry...?" I was never going to get to hear those vows, was I? The kid next to me was fidgeting something awful. His father told him to sit still, but the kid just squirmed more. "Pa, I have to go," he said in an agonized whisper. "Well go on then," his father told him. "But hurry back, and don't go playing around."

The kid stood up and said, "Excuse me, I have to..."

I said, "I know. Please, go." I twisted my knees to the side so he could get by. Lord, there must have been something solid in that fart, because he trailed fumes like a leaky oil tanker trails a slick.

"Do you, Harry, take Samantha, to love, honor..." Oh no. Now the kid was standing in the aisle trying to get his father's attention.

"Pa, there ain't any paper," he hissed.

His father just sat there looking at his kid.

"If anyone sees just cause why Samantha and Harry should not marry, let them now speak or forever hold their peace." Sophie opened her purse and handed the kid a couple of tissues.

"By the power vested in me, I now..."

The three white-haired ladies in front of us were fidgeting now. The middle one turned around to face us. "I thought this was going to be my brother's funeral," she said with tears in her eyes. "Who are these people? Where's my beloved brother?"

"...pronounce you, Samantha and Harry, man and wife."

"I have no idea where your brother is," Sophie said. "I didn't even know he was dead."

"Please kiss the bride," the preacher said almost mournfully. He sure didn't seem to be enjoying himself much. But Harry and Sam didn't seem to notice. Harry put his arms around his bride. She put her arms around his neck and they kissed. They kissed some more. They just kept on kissing. I said, "Sophie, I wish my vacuum had a suction like that."

The white-haired lady twisted back around in her pew and complained, "Somebody should throw some water on those two. That's a disgraceful way to behave in church. And where in hell is my brother?"

Sam and Harry just kept on kissing. The kid came back, his eyes glued to the scene on the altar.

In trying to squeeze past Sophie, he somehow managed to stomp on her meanest corn. She let out a yelp. "I should have let that little son of a bitch shit in his pants," she said.

Finally the two broke their lip-lock and came down the aisle. Sam was practically skipping with happiness. Well, I missed most of the wedding, but I guess they really did it. A huge smile broke out on my face. We all ran outside, except for Sophie, who was limping with pain. We joined the group of people who were waiting to greet the newly married couple. We hugged and kissed Samantha and Harry, who were smiling so hugely I was worried their faces would break in two. I hugged Sam again, and whispered in her ear, "I can't believe you finally tied the knot! I am so unbelievably happy for you."

Tears welled in her eyes, and then she brushed her veil back and said, "Oh, silly, what did you think I was here for? A barbecue?" She laughed, and before I could say anything else to her, I was moved along by the crowd of well wishers.

Sophie, who had one shoe on and the other tucked under her arm, whipped the camera from her purse and took at least six rolls of film. When the entire picture taking was exhausted, Sophie opened her bag and took out a bag of rice that looked big enough to feed everyone in Asia.

Sam and Harry waved and threw kisses as they headed to their car, which now was lavishly decorated. I had wondered what had taken Ralph so long to make it to the alter. Seems he had talked a couple of fellows into helping him with the shaving cream and other accouterments of the traditional wedding car decor. The back window proclaimed "Just Married" in huge letters, and a string of cans about three blocks long trailed behind them in the dust as they pulled out and headed down the road.

Just as I was wondering what her parents were going to do for transportation back to their hotel, I heard the Cadillac roar back up the road to the church, cans clanging on the road and horn blowing. Sam's parents, who were standing off by themselves on the side of the yard, looked mortified, but they climbed into the car, and it took off again down the road. Sam's mother had looked like she swallowed a pickle whole when she saw her beautiful Caddie pulling strings of cans with the back window sprayed and big red-and-white crepe paper bows taped on the rear windows. Tacky, tacky. Knowing what a tricky rascal Ralph can be, I couldn't help but wonder if he did it just for the purpose of busting her Mother's royal ass.

Ralph came over and finally noticed Sophie's half-shod condition. "Sophie, why are you wearing one shoe?"

"Later, Ralph."

"Okay, you can tell me when you're good and ready, but for now will you please put the shoe on so I can take some pictures of you two lovely girls?"

She grimaced, but managed to get the shoe back on and even smiled as Ralph took our picture.

Chapter 25

We got back into the car and started the trip back to our motel. Sophie had her shoe off again and was rubbing her toe. Ralph asked again what the problem was, so I told him the whole story on the drive back. He laughed so hard that tears started pouring down his face. "Who would have guessed it?" he said. "Getting gas blasted in church!" He chuckled for a while, than finally sobered up.

He reached one hand over from the steering wheel and put it on Sophie's knee. "Remember the day we were married, what we did after the reception?" He looked at me in the rearview mirror. "We drove to Atlantic City, but we never made it to the boardwalk. The room, which was a really nice one facing the ocean, cost ten dollars a night, but we sure did get our money's worth out of it, eh Soph?" She took his hand off her knee and placed it back on the steering wheel, obviously getting annoyed. "She had me locked in there for two days. You took such advantage of me, didn't you, honey? Listen, when we get back to the motel, would you like me to kiss your toe, make it better? Maybe massage your back? If you relax, the pain will go bye bye."

"Are you getting horny?" She turned to me and said, "Weddings do that to Ralph."

"Now that you mention it, I do feel a little peculiar," he said.

Okay, now I was feeling uncomfortable. To change the subject, I asked Ralph if he didn't think that preacher looked like an undertaker.

"You're right," he replied, "he is an undertaker, but he was a preacher first. He decided he could make more money burying people than marrying them."

"Now how would you know that?" I asked.

"Well, we had a little time to kill up there on the altar while we were waiting for Sam, so I chatted a bit with the man," Ralph said.

"Years back, the old undertaker was really getting old, so during the week this preacher would go help him embalm the dead, dress them, whatever was necessary. When the old undertaker died, he just took over the business, and the church got a new preacher. When the regular preacher gets laid, eh hem, laid up, with gout, the undertaker does the preaching."

"How old is the preacher that has gout?" I asked. Hey, it was a better topic than Ralph's horniness.

Ralph laughed. "He's about fifty years old but gout is not really his problem. When he goes out Saturday night and gets a real good snoot full and then gets lucky, they just tell the parishioners his gout flared up again. He gets his recreational relaxation at the motel where we are staying. In fact, early this morning when I was getting my decorations together, I saw him leaving."

I was starting to think he was pulling my leg. "Ralph, how can you know all this? You don't even live here."

"When I was washing the car this morning Skipper gave me the scoop on all major happenings. For example, those four guys who came in while you were eating breakfast? Skipper said that they have a good reason to stay at the motel instead of in town like most guys who come into the area on business or on a stopover. About eleven at night a car full of local hookers come to their rooms for a couple of hours."

"And Margaret puts up with this?" I said incredulously. She didn't seem like the type who would enjoy operating a bordello.

"His wife has no idea," Ralph said. "That guy has a good business. He charges 35 a night, including breakfast. What the girls charge is their business. Besides, I saw him leaving a room down at the end where we are staying about six this morning. They have a nice place, but how do you think they could stay in business if they only got customers from the traffic that comes down that dirt road every day? He said that some days, he'll only have one car stop for two dollars worth of gas. Just think of it as a different kind of pumping station." This talk seemed to get him back around to the previous conversation. I was sorry I got him started.

"Sophie, would you like to fool around—I mean let me make your toe better?"

She said, "You dirty old man," but I could tell she was softening up with all the sweet talk. Ralph was really good at what he was doing. For sure he was going to get his plan to happen.

"Sophie, you have never looked lovelier than you do today. In fact, if the desire I feel for you was electricity, tonight I could light up all of Macon."

Thankfully, we were pulling up in front of the motel. I hopped out, leaving them in the car to rev up whatever motor they wanted. "How soon should I be ready?" I asked over my shoulder as I headed off to my room.

"Better make it an hour and a half," Ralph said. "Sophie is in serious pain."

Missy was sitting by my door as I walked up. She solemnly held out her paw for me to shake.

"Hi, sweet girl," I said, ruffling her fur. "Come on in. You can tell me about your day—and about what goes on here at night." I noticed a jar of home-made peach preserves sitting on the dresser. That was a very nice thought, but right then I was so thirsty the preserves would just stick in my throat. I needed to change, but first I needed something to cool my parched throat. I had noticed a Coke machine tucked away between the rooms just a few doors down. I got a handful of change and went to the machine. Before I could put the money in the slot, I heard Margaret's voice.

"I was just coming down here and saw you at the machine. Would you like a cold glass of iced tea with a big wedge of lemon instead?"

"Sounds great," I said thankfully. "Certainly a lot better than a can of soda. Let me come up with you and get it." She said she wouldn't hear of it; she'd go fetch it and bring it to my room. What a nice woman, I thought as I headed back to my room. She was so warm, and quite attractive, too. With the air of good breeding she had about her, I could only imagine what she would think if she ever found out about the nightly activity going on around her.

She knocked on the door, and then pushed in with a glass filled with iced tea and a large wedge of lemon. I took a sip, and sighed.

"Margaret that is the best iced tea I ever had. Thank you for it, and for the peach preserves." She said it was nothing, invited me over to the kitchen for some pie, and headed back out again. Missy looked at me with hopeful eyes, so I gave her an ice cube. She hopped up on the bed and lay down, happily crunching the ice between her teeth.

I took another big sip of the tea, than began

changing into more casual clothing. As I was hanging up my dress, I heard Ralph's voice through the wall to the next room yelling "Yippee." I didn't want to think about why. As I turned on the shower, I heard the water begin to run next door. Then I heard Ralph sing three verses of "I'm Back in the Saddle Again."

"Thank you, folks," I heard him say when he finished singing. "That was a favorite tune of one of my old-time favorite Western singing cowboys, Gene Autry, coming live to you from one of his fans here in the back roads of Macon." Now I knew that all men react differently to getting their ashes hauled, but that Ralph was really weird.

Then he pounded on the bedroom wall and yelled, "Are you ready? Let's get the bus loaded and roll." I pounded back and yelled I'd meet them out by the car. He didn't seem to know he didn't need to yell to be heard through the wall, and I decided not to disillusion him. I finished getting dressed, called Missy and headed back out into the afternoon heat. I stopped by the kitchen and thanked Margaret again for her hospitality. I could smell the fresh-baked pies she had sitting on the windowsill. She again offered me a piece, and was I tempted to sit down and have a bite, but Ralph and Sophie were probably already waiting for me by the car, so I had to decline her kind invitation. Missy, however, was glad to take her up on it, and as I walked out the door, I could hear her slurping up some of the ambrosial apple pie. Maybe later I could join her, I thought, though I generally prefer to eat at a table instead of off a plate on the floor.

Sure enough, Ralph and Sophie were already by the car, to go to the wedding reception, looking a little flushed and silly. Sophie was fanning herself with the fan she got from the church, and Ralph kept on hitching up his belt. Give me a break, I thought. They just had to flaunt it in front of a poor girl who'd been in a dry spell for quite some time now.

"How far is it to the nursing home?" I asked, opening the door. A blast furnace of heat whapped me in the face, and I stepped back for a moment to let the hot air out of the car. "Seems like the Southern way to gauge mileage is 'down the road a piece' or 'just over the hill' and you'll get there God willing and the creek don't rise."

"Still can't believe you got gas-blasted in church," Ralph said with a snicker. "At least it wasn't that poor old biddie in front of you looking for her dead brother. That would have really been bad."

"Please spare me," I replied. "Nothing could have been worse than that kid's fart."

"Well now," Sophie said, "that's not strictly true. Old people have a lot of gas. Their teeth get loose, then they only half chew the food and swallow a lot of air. Like my neighbor, Alice. When she comes over, I have to keep her in the kitchen where the chairs are made of vinyl." At my questioning look, she explained, "One time I let her sit in the living room while we had coffee and cake. My poor new sofa has never been the same; it's smelled like an outhouse ever since. The only thing about keeping her in the kitchen is that I have to keep her back end aimed away from the gas stove—otherwise she could blow up the house." Sophie shifted in her seat, getting warmed up to her topic.

"That Alice is amazing, though. Eighty-seven and she still likes to talk about sex every chance she gets. She told me she would like to have it real good one more time before she either goes six feet under or into a mental blank and not know what's happening.

"She had a fellow coming around last year, but he could hardly get up her steps, much less into her bedroom. He was history after just a couple of visits. She said they tried, but his poor old pecker looked like an old veteran laying on two duffel bags." Sophie laughed.

"Ralph, do you remember those white plastic ducks you bought me to plant flowers in? I had them on the porch one day when Alice stopped by. She said, 'Sophie, where the hell did you get those ugly white plastic ducks?' I told her Ralph bought those for me at a flower shop. "The hell he did," she said. "I got those at a flea market for two bucks apiece, and then sold them to some fellow who lives a couple blocks away at my yard sale for three bucks apiece. His wife had a yard sale a week later, and that's where Ralph bought them." Well, I should have known something was up. "Remember, Ralph, when you gave those plastic ducks to me you said that now I would have something nobody else would have?"

"Well, you must admit, Sophie, that was the truth," Ralph said.

"I remember when Sam came by and saw those ducks on my porch," Sophie continued. "I told her I wasn't sure what I was going to do with them. They were really ugly. Sam said I should take them to the cemetery; maybe someone would do me a favor and steal them." Then, as always, Sophie's thoughts soon turned to food.

"Ralph, I thought we were going to have a piece of that bodacious homemade apple pie and coffee when we came from church," she said.

He laughed, "Those were my plans, but I got laid—I mean waylaid—by your far more luscious temptations, honey. The decision was one made in a fever of necessity."

Sophie looked at Ralph. "You keep talking all this bullshit and pretty soon you will have yourself believing your stories."

"Oh, but it's so true, my love. I am the Tarzan man swinging through your jungle of love."

And I was a woman who was about to gag.

Sophie giggled, but fortunately, Ralph had to start paying attention to the road or he'd never find the reception site.

Chapter 26

He turned at a white arrow sign, and we drove down a one-lane road haloed with trees covered with hanging moss. As we came around a curve, we saw a huge, white house, standing proud straight ahead of us.

"A mansion converted to a house of welcome," said Ralph. "Looks like we've arrived. Just remember, Sophie, whatever I do will be in fun."

"Yes, Ralph. And you remember that what's good for the goose is good for the gander."

"If you two don't behave yourselves, both the goose and gander will be cooked," I said. We all laughed and exited the car.

Chapter 27

As we entered the grounds, I noticed it had a wide, wrap around porch that seemed to embrace the beautiful old house like a pair of loving arms holding all the stories and memories it must have collected over the years. A large sign standing to the left of the lawn informed us that this was indeed the Prickly Pines Rest Home.

We parked under one of the many pines near the drive, noting that the needles were indeed prickly. Not too prickly, I hoped. The last thing we needed was another flat tire. As we approached the porch we were greeted by a very stern-looking woman who let us know right off the bat just who was in charge.

"I am Emma Mae Norton," she informed us, "and you are all welcome to share our facilities for the reception."

She escorted us to the largest room in the house, which already was accommodating about twelve guests. One was in a wheelchair, two had walkers, and all were wearing big smiles. They looked like they were ready to party. Except for one elderly gentleman who was sitting on what looked to be a black inner tube. When I asked him about it, he said

he had just had a hemorrhoid operation, and needed to sit on the tube for cushioning. He looked
uncomfortable, and I felt sorry for him. What awful
thing to put up with at a shindig blast like this one
no doubt would be?

There were long tables set up on either side of
the room, and chairs scattered about. I looked out
the oversized windows that lined one wall of the
room, and I could see cars pulling up and people
carrying large pots and deep dishes full of food.
Within a short time the long tables that were so bare
now looked to be too small to hold all the goodies
that kept coming in with each new wave of arrivals.
The place was starting to fill up as well, with all
kinds of people. Young and old, men and women,
some dressed in their Sunday best, while others
came in jeans. I heard one man ask if anyone
thought to bring something good to drink. "Don't
worry, Bubba," he replied, "we have plenty."

Just then a hand touched my arm. I looked up
and saw a beautiful woman of about 40 dressed in a
plain cotton shift. She asked me to come with her to
the kitchen, where all the large kettles were being
taken for heating. The kitchen contained two large
stoves, which already were covered to capacity with
cooking pots.

"Here, honey, help me with this," she said. I
grabbed the other handle of the enormous boiler
she was lugging, and we swung it up onto one of the

stovetops. She began stirring the kettle's contents with a ladle that was as long as my arm. I said, "It smells good. What is it?"

"Road kill," she replied, scraping up bits from the bottom of the pot.

"Oh really. I don't believe I have ever had that," I said, mystified. She couldn't really mean road kill, could she?

She laughed, revealing a smile that was missing more than a few teeth. "No, Missy, from that Northern accent of yours, I don't believe you have. But y'all are in for a treat. I make the best road kill in the county. Just last week, Jed collected me a nice possum, two squirrels, and a coon off Route 23. Now that's good eating. I'll make sure you get a fair portion when it gets hot, because it goes fast."

The faster the better, in my opinion. "That's very kind of you," I said politely, "however, just make sure everyone has a very fair portion, I can wait. In fact, I can always get some the next time I come by here." I left her by her pot and went back into the main reception area.

A woman in a sea-green coat came in, and everyone gave a roar of greeting, and an even louder one when her husband followed her in with a giant boiler. He was telling everyone the pot was very hot, to give him some space to get the pot placed on the table. I heard someone say, "Bertha, if that cooking pot is full, you made enough chicken bog for the Confederate army."

Didn't anyone just bring some cheese and crackers? I thought, remembering Sam's reaction to my serving her Spagetti-Os. I'd even take Spagetti-Os about then.

Then a white-bearded man with an odd accent, who I later learned was from Baton Rouge, Louisiana, came through with a large boiler, announcing that he had in his hands his world-famous dirty rice. "Oh, dear God," I murmured under my breath.

Sophie came over just then and rescued me. She grabbed my arm and pulled me over to the other side of the room, saying, "I want you to meet Sam's Memaw and Pepaw."

As I approached these two people I had heard so many wonderful stories about, I looked at them and thought, what a handsome man and lovely woman. They smiled and both extended their arms to enclose me.

After the hugs I told them I was Megan, then looked at these two precious people, still holding their hand and told them how much I have looked forward to meeting both of them. Sam loves you both very much—but why am I telling you something you already know?"

They seemed to know quite a bit about me as well. Seems Sam talked a lot about me to them by phone and mail. We all agreed that Sam was an unusual and very special person. Sam had many of her Memaw's features: her high cheek bones, bright blue eyes, and a smile that made you wonder just what she was up to this time. Funny how all these traits seemed to have jumped a generation. While Sam's mother had the cheekbones, she had none of Memaw's mischievous charm. I glanced around, but didn't see Sam's mother anywhere. Her father either. I thought this was a little odd, but I was so thrilled to meet Memaw and Pepaw, I let it pass out of my mind.

Pepaw was a tall man with the build of someone who worked hard on the farm most of his life. When he held my hand, I could feel the hardened, scarred skin of his palms scratching against mine. Memaw and Pepaw looked so happy together that I thought they must love each other very much. Then Pepaw excused himself to help the new arrivals, who came bearing yet more kettles full of God knows what.

Memaw said, "You will never know how happy you made Sam and Harry by coming to their wedding, and how happy you made me by coming to the reception to share this special day with us." She saw my incredulous look as I glanced sideways at the groaning tables and the homespun clothing of the women ladling out their specialties.

"You know, we are not as back woodsy as we all may seem," she said. "Some like the city life, but Grant and I always liked the country and farming."

"What is your name? Besides Memaw, I mean."

"It's Elizabeth."

"I am not very good at remembering names; but I shall remember yours."

"Why is that?"

"Because that's my middle name Megan, Elizabeth" I told her.

She laughed, and cast a loving glance at her husband. "Will you look at Grant? He has an ulterior motive in helping those folks with their food; he wants to check out what they made. He always had a good appetite. Thankfully, he worked so hard, he never got fat."

"I'm sure you were very busy with raising a family, cooking, and doing all the canning," I said. "Sam told me all about how much work there was to do on the farm, plus you had to feed two farm hands."

She sighed. "Oh, those were wonderful days, those summers Sam stayed with us. She is a wonderful girl. I just hope she will be as happy as she deserves. Did Sam, in all her stories about us, tell you I was an RN?"

Surprised, I said, "No, Sam never told me that." She laughed. "Guess she must have forgotten."

"Where did you work as a registered nurse?" I asked. "I mean, was there a hospital near your farm?"

"No, my dear, you misunderstood. Around here, an RN is a racing nut. Whenever the car races, motorcycle races were near enough for me to get there, you better believe I found a way to see them. Then they started to show the races on the TV. That's when I told Grant we had to get one of those machines. It's not the same on the TV, though. You have to be there and smell the exhaust to really get the feel for it."

I was enjoying our conversation, but several more people were coming to visit with Elizabeth, so I decided to mix with the rest of the crowd and talk with her more later. Plus, I wanted to find Sam and Harry. I didn't think they'd arrived yet, but with the room so crowded, it was hard to tell.

I found my eyes kept being drawn back to those tables of chow. I noticed that the end of one small table didn't have any food on it, but was instead full of Mason jars filled with water. Why would you have water in screw-top Mason jars, I wondered.

My curiosity was soon to be fulfilled. Ralph materialized at my side and handed me a small paper cup full of water from the jars. He said, "Sam and Harry just pulled up. We're going to toast them." Moments later, the door burst open and Sam and Harry came in. Sam looked gorgeous, wearing that black-and-white number she had bought at that funky little shop during our shopping trip in the Village. Everyone and I mean everyone, raised his or her cup toward the couple, and then drank.

I didn't feel anything for a second, and then it was like I swallowed molten gold. I could feel my stockings melting, and the entire lining of my throat was beyond repair. I was unable to utter a sound. I heard a ringing in my head that sounded like a fire alarm, but no one was running for the exits, so it must have been internal. I shook my head to clear it.

Gasping for breath, I looked around. Everyone else appeared to be in a normal state. It took several minutes before I had voice and breath enough to whisper harshly to Ralph, "What was that I just drank?"

"Homemade moonshine. Some call it white lightning."

"I can see why," I retorted. "Are you trying to get rid of me or something? I would like to stay and enjoy this party, but that lightning bolt almost did me in." Ralph just laughed at me.

Later on, someone offered me some homemade peach wine. That sounded safe, so I tried it. Unlike the moonshine, it was really good and soothed my still-raw throat. Everyone was having a grand time. An eighty-two-year-old house resident was manning the piano, pounding out some raucous tunes. Everyone was dancing and singing along. Once the peach wine made friends with the high-octane I previously drank, I joined in.

As I shimmied around the dance floor, I saw that the hemorrhoid man was looking much happier. He was now up dancing with his rubber tube on his head. It looked like Firestone's version of a halo.

One of the sweet old ladies in a wheelchair who greeted us as we came in now was sitting near the piano player and belting out "Carolina Moon Keep Shining."

Just then someone announced that the band had arrived. The guitar, banjo, and fiddle players reeled into the room raring to go. They seemed so enthusiastic that I was certain they got a little help from the brown crock with a large cork, which they carried in like it was a basket of eggs, careful not to drop their precious cargo. The white-bearded, dirty rice man from Louisiana said, "Here, let me help you with that," and grabbed for the crock.

"You gotta pay if you want to play," the guitar player said, pulling the jar away from him.

The Louisiana man said, "No problem," and reached down to open a black case by his feet. He pulled out a clarinet and blew a few notes.

"Hot damn, you're good," said the guitar player, handing him the crock. "welcome to the band."

They may have been retired, but let me tell you, those boys could play. I could have danced to that music with both legs in a cast. It may have been the peach wine, but I was feeling fine. I could still feel my upper lip, which I took as a sign that I could have another glass when I took a break. While there wasn't an excessive amount of moon shine being consumed, it did not take a lot; that was some potent stuff. They should hand out a glass or two with dinner, and the dear residents of this place would never have to take a sleeping pill again.

When Sam had first told me about the reception being in a rest home, I thought it was a daffy idea.

Rest homes were always such quiet places. Now, as I stomped and whirled, I wondered why all rest homes didn't have music like this. There is no greater enemy than silence, and no greater friend than a tune that gets your blood up.

I finally caught another glimpse of Sam and Harry on the other side of the dancers. They were so happy I could feel the love radiating like a beam from them. They were dancing, kissing, and smiling to each other like this was the first best day of their new life. I had managed to grab Sam for a few minutes, but there was no way we could really talk during the reception. They were going to Florida for their honeymoon yes, driving the rental full of family heirlooms and dragging their pickup behind them, believe it or not. Sam said she'd call me when they got there.

Then a big, barrel-chested man wearing a white turtleneck, a denim jacket, jeans, and cowboy boots came into this room. At six foot two, he almost seemed to hover over the crowd. The merriment and noise died down as people spotted him. He stood there for a moment, just looking around, then smiled and walked over to Sam. He grabbed her around the waist with one arm, and then gave her a kiss right on the mouth. And it was not a good friend peck, let me tell you. The tension in the room got pretty heavy before the band broke it up by swinging into a new song. He must have asked Sam to dance, because, after she turned and said a few words to Harry, she went out onto the dance floor with him.

Harry walked over to me, looking like a little boy who's favorite toy just got run over by the family station wagon. "That's that high-school sweetheart Sam told me about," he said, scuffing his shoe on the floor. "She told me all about how he thought they would get married when they graduated from high school. Seems the whole town thought they would, too. Sam told me she liked him a lot, but like she said, he was the one talking marriage, not her. She cared about him, but she wanted to, as she put it, 'do her own thing' for a while first. Then her father was transferred up North, so nothing ever came of it." He looked out at his bride dancing with her old boyfriend. "Looks like she still enjoys his company, though doesn't it?"

I put my hand on Harry's shoulder. "You know that Sam's had a few boyfriends in the past, Harry. She's even come close to the altar before. But don't ever doubt this: She made her choice today. You are the man she married. You are the one she wants to spend her life with. Let her dance with that high-school memory. She may have thought he was the right thing for her many years ago. But this is now, and you are the main man." I crossed my fingers behind my back, hoping what I had just said wasn't a lie.

Harry looked at me and smiled. "May I have this dance?"

We danced some more, but I had to beg off after a while. I wanted another glass of the peach wine to knock down my thirst, and I was so hungry I could have taken a bite out of my own rear end. I hadn't eaten anything since breakfast, I suddenly realized. I filled another paper cup, swilled down the nectar, and looked up again to see Sam's big chest former boyfriend coming my way.

"Well, I hear you came from the big city up north for the wedding," he said. "What are you, a teacher or something?"

"No. I make reversible skates for backward children," was my smart mouth reply. No doubt about it that jelly jar moonshine and the wine were taking over my tongue. That plus I was none too pleased to see a former flame of Sam's hanging around.

He turned away in disgust, and that was the last I saw of him. The banjo player yelled for quiet then made an announcement. "We are going to take a break and eat, but before we do the band wants to toast Sam and Harry. You all join us."

Out came the Mason jars full of clear liquid, and some was poured into the small paper cups for everyone. Luckily, I was standing next to a planter. As all raised their cups I discretely deposited mine into the ferns.

Looking up, I finally spotted Sam's parents on the other side of the room. Her mother was talking with Memaw and Pepaw, and she looked almost relaxed and—dare I say it, happy. Her father was over in a corner talking with what looked to be an old friend. How nice for him that he got a chance to hook up with some of his cronies from back when they used to live around here, I thought. Sam's mother seemed to disagree. She happened to glance in his direction, then stalked away from Memaw and Pepaw in a huff. She grabbed his arm and dragged him outside. That moonshine sure has a strange effect on people I thought.

Finally, time to eat. I was so hungry that the road-kill stew smelled mighty fine. Fortunately, I didn't have to go that far. They had the best fried chicken I ever tasted, and macaroni and cheese. I tried the collards, the butter beans, and some of the black-eyed peas with chunks of bacon. The corn-bread also was heavenly. The desserts were lethal, but luscious; I had the pecan pie and peach cobbler.

When I finished stuffing myself, I went out to the porch and sat down on one of the rockers. The sun would soon be setting, and the grounds looked lovely in the soft light. The Spanish moss hanging from the trees looked majestic, and the lovely magnolias scented the air. It truly was another world. I vowed to myself that someday I would return to the South and spend more time. I relaxed into the rocker, moving it a little with my feet. The music and laughter coming from inside were comforting.

Sam and Harry came out and announced they were leaving. The hordes of people streamed out behind them, overflowing the porch and ending up on the lawn. I kissed them both and said, "Be happy. I'll see you back in New Jersey. And drive safely— no sleeping in the truck, right, Harry?"

Harry laughed and pulled Sam close to him. "Not to worry on that account," he said. "I doubt we'll do much sleeping anywhere, right, Sam?"

She giggled like a schoolgirl, then hugged me again and whispered, "I'm so glad you came." Then they pushed through the crowd to their car, and drove away, the cans still tied to strings on the rear bumper as they drove down the long, dusty, dirt country road. I wondered how long the crepe paper streaming from the aerial would last.

Most folks lingered outside for a while, enjoying the slightly cooler but definitely fresher air. Then we heard a scream coming from inside and we all went to check out what was happening. Seems there was a pantry room off the kitchen where racks of pies and cakes were waiting for the next day's desserts for the residents. Early morning, the cook had left several home-baked lemon meringue pies on pie shelves in the pantry. She had gone to check on them before heading home for the night, when she saw a field mouse stuck smack in the middle of one of the pie's meringue, and this poor little bugger was struggling for his life to get free.

The banjo player took the pie and sat it on the kitchen table. We all gathered around here was the dilemma: Should we throw the pie away with the mouse in it or get the mouse out, wash it off and set it free, then throw out the pie? Now remember, the jury in the case of the meringue mouse was for all intents and purposes, three sheets to the wind. I personally voted to get the mouse out alive and get on with the celebration. The vote was unanimous: the mouse would live.

The piano player got a pair of tongs from his truck and carefully picked out the mouse. Still holding it with the tongs, he took it outside, washed it off with the garden hose, and set it free. We all seemed to breathe a sigh of relief. Everyone who had come out to observe the sentence being carried out now felt in desperate need of a beverage to celebrate the happy ending, so we all trooped back inside.

They broke out the paper cups again and filled them with assorted beverages, and the music and dancing started up again. Emma Mae Norton, the hostess who greeted us so stiffly at the top of the steps when we arrived, sat on top of the piano, wearing a baseball cap she swiped from some guy named Charlie backwards on her head. She leaned over and sang "I Can't Give You Anything But Love, Baby," to the clarinet player, who rewarded her with a solo.

I don't know what time the reception finally came to a halt, but it had to be after one in the morning. Frankly, had I been wearing a watch, I am not certain I could have read the hands anyway.

Chapter 28

Somehow we got back to the car and started driving down the dark, bumpy, dirt road at a speed way beyond the fifty miles per hour that Ralph swore he was never going to exceed on the trip down. The moon was full, but the night still seemed awfully dark to me, much darker than it would have seemed back home. We were the only car on the road, and I almost felt like the heroine in one of those scary movies. Something flashed through the headlights as it ran across the road, and Sophie let out a scream. Ralph told her that it was only a fox going home from a late party, just like we were. Finally, I saw the lights from our motel, and that was one welcome sight, let me tell you.

There were quite a few cars parked at the motel, but hardly any lights were on in the rooms. Sophie said, "They must be busy tonight." I saw a car that looked familiar to me. I wasn't sure, but I thought it was the car Sam's father's friend had driven away from the reception in. That's strange, I thought groggily. I had heard from someone or other that he still lived around here, so why would he be staying at the motel? I glanced at the few windows that were still lit, and thought I caught a glimpse of a profile that looked a lot like Sam's father. All that wine and dancing must have me hallucinating, I thought. Sam's parents were staying at a hotel several miles in the other direction.

I rubbed my hand across my eyes and climbed out of the car wearily. I could already feel a bit of a headache coming on. "Good night, Sophie, good night, Ralph. If I live through the rest of the night, I'll see you two in the morning."

"Don't forget, we're leaving first thing in the morning," Ralph said. "I'll see you at six."

"Not if I see you first," I said, and crawled off to my room. I sat on the end of the bed in my air-cooled room, and then fell back. That's all I remember.

Chapter 29

It couldn't have been more than an hour that passed before I heard a knock on my door. Then another. Then a regular marching band was pounding at the door.

"Rise and shine," I heard Ralph's disgustingly cheerful voice say. "Give you half an hour to get ready." I groaned and pulled the pillow over my face, then looked out the window. Ralph and Sophie were packing their things into the trunk. The sunlight hurt my eyes, and I turned my head back to the dimness of the room. I felt like hell: My head hurt, and my mouth felt like the Marine Corps had marched across my tongue wearing combat boots.

Three aspirin, a shower, and half a bottle of mouthwash gave me temporary recovery. I was on my way to becoming human again.

Then I heard another knock. "Come on, girl," Ralph said. "We're ready to roll." I sent a few nasty thoughts in his direction. Trust me, he deserved every one. I counted to ten, then opened the doors and shoved my suitcases outside.

Ralph grabbed my bags and strode over to the car, where he began stashing them in the trunk. I emerged. Sophie said, "You don't look so good, girl.

What you need is a good breakfast. We will stop to eat at a place about an hour from here."

"Sophie, shut it down before I barf on your shoes," I said as I climbed into my assigned space in the backseat and thought about the long drive home.

Ralph turned the key, but nothing happened. He slapped the wheel and tried again, this time getting a horrible grinding noise. He got out of the car and raised the hood, then stood staring at the engine like it held the secrets of the universe. Sophie stuck her head out the window and told Ralph to do something. Ralph complied by starting to curse a blue streak. I leaned my head back against the seat, just wanting to be home already. The car's not the only thing that's out of order, I thought, feeling last night's wine. I was about to either throw up or faint. Either would have been preferable to my current state, I thought.

It was getting hotter by the damn minute, as Sophie and I crawled out of the car. I stood there, swaying gently back and forth, before I thought to sit down on the grass before I passed out. Sophie was getting irritable, and started snapping at Ralph, who was poking around under the hood. Finally, Ralph gave up and told us he was going inside the motel to call Luke, a good old boy Ralph had met at the reception, who knew everything about cars. He went into the kitchen to round up a phone.

Just then a truck pulled up. It was Sam's old, big-chested boyfriend from the reception, looking all too chipper in cut-off jeans, a sweatshirt with short sleeves, construction boots, and heavy white socks.

"Howdy, folks!" he boomed. "Ready to leave for home?"

"We're ready, but the car doesn't seem to be willing and able," Sophie said.

"Well, now, let me have a look here," he said, his head disappearing into the bowels of the engine. He did something in there, then raised his head over the hood of the car and said, "Missy, you get behind the wheel."

I followed Big Chest's wishes. He might not have been my favorite person, but I'd do anything just to get the hell out of here. I would have kissed King Kong's ass in Macy's window if it would get the car started.

"Now, girl. Crank it."

I was perspiring freely, my hands sweaty on the steering wheel. What the hell did he mean, "crank it"? He looked at me over the hood and again repeated the instructions to "crank it." I just sat there in a stupor. He came over to the open car and looked at me, sweat beginning to stream down his face. He reached into the car, tapped the key said, "Put your foot on the gas and crank it."

"Oh, you mean start it. Why the hell didn't you

just say that in the first place?" I said, turning the key. I did not like him the night before, and that morning I was positive I couldn't stand him. His face was getting red, and I could tell he was getting angry. Well that made two of us. No matter how hard I "cranked it," the engine refused to turn over.

I told Big Chest about the trouble we had coming down with the car hesitating. He diagnosed the problem as dirt in the gas line and said we needed a new gas filter. "I reckon you ain't never gonna get one on Sunday," he added.

Ralph came out, squinting in the bright sun, and said that Luke would be there around noon. Okay, we had several hours to kill. I reckoned we were going in for breakfast. After all, sitting around a table and eating seemed to be Ralph and Sophie's solution to every problem. By the time they were finished with the meal, they seemed to think, all your problems would be solved. Absolution through eggs: who would have guessed?

We all trooped into the kitchen and let Margaret fix us some breakfast. I managed to get through a biscuit without throwing up, which I felt was a major feat. The food did help my hangover, though.

As promised, Luke showed up around noon. The hood went up once again. He poked around, than tried to "crank it." Still no luck. Luke agreed with Big Chest's opinion that it was gas-line dirt and that it needed a new gas filter. Unfortunately, he also agreed that the problem wasn't going to be fixed that day. "Them kinda stores are closed on Sundays," he informed us. Looked like we were stuck there for another night.

We took what we needed from the trunk and stashed our bags in our rooms. I just wanted to go back to bed. Sophie and Ralph were about as friendly as wildcats, and I was not enjoying their company at the moment, to be perfectly honest.

I went up to the house and sat down at the big kitchen table. I slumped in my chair and put my head in my hands. Margaret materialized with a glass of sweet tea. She set it before me, and I gulped it down.

Must have been the ice: My headache came back with a vengeance. "I've got just the thing for what ails y'all," Margaret said when I grimaced and rubbed my hand over my forehead. She brought me a glass of tomato juice with fresh lemon. I held the glass to my face for a moment, feeling the cool beads of water that had condensed on the sides, then took a sip. It did seem to help some.

I told Margaret that I reckon I really wanted to get back home, and our chances were looking slim of my getting there any time soon. Being the sweet lady she was, she told me now don't you fret none, everything would be fine; just when you think things are darn right messed up something good happens and the whole mess just goes away. Just think about what you want most and it will happen

"Fine" wasn't working for me. How would I get home to New Jersey in time to get myself squared away for the meetings on Tuesday morning? Would I live to see New Jersey again?

Ralph came into the kitchen and took pity on me. "Girl, you look like you're in a pretty bad way," he said. He put his hand on my shoulder and gave me the Southern blessing, "Don't you fret none". "We will be on our way sometime tomorrow." But I wasn't buying it.

Maybe I could catch a plane home. There had to be an airport somewhere in this state, right? "Margaret, do you have a phone book?" I asked.

"Sorry, darlin', I never did have one of those."

"What do you want with a phone book?" Ralph asked.

"I was thinking I could call the airport and find out about flights. Maybe I could just call a cab to take me to the airport, and I could be home by tomorrow night."

"Are you crazy, girl? You can't just call a cab to come pick you up here in the middle of nowhere. Nearest airport is probably in Atlanta, which would be at least an hour and a half's drive. Even if you could get a cab out here, do you have any idea how much that would cost? Why not just call the Atlanta airport, have them come for you by plane? They could land that old jet right here on the county road." He sighed. "Better settle yourself down and get used to the idea that it'll be a bit before you get home."

"You couldn't call a cab anyway," Margaret added helpfully. "You can only make local calls from here." Great. The phone company must have gone by this area on a broom if all you can do is make calls to folks up and down this rutted, dusty road.

"Besides," Ralph said, "Luke invited us to the church today for a pig-picking party and games. He says it starts at one and usually lasts until the pig is gone."

"What is a pig-picking?" I asked, becoming resigned to the fact that my fate was to be exposed to every strange Southern ritual there could be before being allowed to go back home.

Margaret, who had been listening in, said, "Gull, you have never been to a pig-picking? It's a Southern tradition. You'll love it. It'll help you get over your fretting."

Oh yeah? Well, I damn well planned to fret all I wanted to, whatever the hell fret meant. I would have been willing to take out a second mortgage on my house to pay for the cab that would get me out of here. These folks must be born with an extra gland that keeps them from fretting. They are so calm about everything. They don't know that Northern folks have the patience of a nat.

Chapter 30

I wandered back outside, than beat a hasty retreat into my room to sulk. It was so freaking, blasted hot down here. Nothing but dust. Not a sign of life except one car stop for gas five hours ago. I was really getting irritable. Then, Ralph really made my day by telling me it was supposed to get even hotter by the afternoon. Ralph was telling me things would be straightened out by morning, not to fret. Bullshit. I was sick of listening to Ralph, who was starting to sound like Scarlet O'Hara with his "Tomorrow is another day" crap. If there is any way for me to get to an airport, I swore to myself that I would find it. By morning I was going to be headed for the Atlanta airport come hell or high water. And screw that old Southern expression, "God willing and the creek don't rise." I was from the North, and there we believe "You damn well better do it yourself or it ain't gonna get done." Okay, so I'd go to the pig-poking or pickling or whatever the hell it was. Maybe I could find someone to ride me down to Atlanta.

I picked myself up off the bed and decided to take another shower. I felt so sticky from the humidity that if a fly had landed on me, it'd be glued there for life.

By the time I had gotten showered and dressed, Luke had already come to pick us up for the picnic. His pickup truck only seated two in the front, maybe three in a pinch. Once Sophie claimed it for herself, though, Ralph and I knew we were consigned to the back of the truck. Ralph gave me a hand up on the tailgate, and we settled in on piles of burlap. At least we'd get some of that famous air-cooling once the truck got under way, I thought.

I hadn't factored in the dust, though. We were dust blasted both, by our own wake, and by the dust trails from the other moving objects on wheels passing like a bat released from hell in the other direction. I had agreed to come along to the picnic at the church because I figured anything would be better than sitting in my air-cooled room with a temperature now hugging ninety. I was wrong. I clung to the hope that it would be worth it, that maybe I'd find some way out of this seventh circle of hell.

I saw a sign for a general store and yelled up to Luke, who was driving like a maniac down the bumpy, dirt road, to pull into the lot.

I climbed up the rickety steps, noting the ubiquitous, big, black pot of boiled peanuts by the door as I passed into the relative coolness of the store. The door was missing the lower half of its screen. As I pushed inside, I was startled by the clang of a cowbell hung over the frame that let the proprietor know when a customer was coming in.

For a small store in the middle of nowhere, it was amazingly well-stocked. There were sections for groceries, hardware, paper goods, and sewing needs. There was a pot-bellied stove near a small-framed window that was almost overshadowed by shutters. A small table and four chairs stood in the corner, with a checkerboard all set up and waiting for someone to sit down and play. A chicken brushed past my legs and cackled as it headed for the screen door. I watched it strut straight through the broken screen. Around the cracker barrel came the fattest cat I had ever seen. Glue strips holding an astounding variety of things that once could fly, twirled lazily overhead. I ducked to make sure that my hair didn't get caught in one of those Venus fly-traps. Just the thought was enough to make my stomach flip-flop. Then I saw it: a pay phone.

A small, gray-haired woman suddenly appeared out of nowhere behind the counter. What, did she have a trap door in the floor so she could appear and disappear like magic? I had given up all expectations at this point: Nothing would have surprised me.

She did have a pleasant smile, though. "What can I get you, gull?" She said.

"Would you have a phone book?"

"You're in luck. I been waiting for the phone man six months to drop this book off on his run," she answered, passing over the book to me. I felt like kissing it. But I didn't. Instead, I turned to the airlines section in the yellow pages. Which one would rescue me and whisk me back to New Jersey? I hit the jackpot on my first call. There was a flight leaving at noon on Monday. I would be in New Jersey by early evening. I said, "Book me." Okay, so that's one problem solved. Now if I could just find a way to get to Atlanta, I'll be all set.

Sophie, who had trailed me inside, bought a couple of moon pies, two bags of fried pork rinds, a bag of boiled peanuts, a couple of Goody Powders for Ralph, and a soda for us all. While we waited for Ralph to finish using the men's room, I said to Sophie, "You know, you have a stomach like that pot in front of the store."

"What do you mean?"

"Cast iron."

I looked down at my feet, and saw that I had almost stepped on a white ball lying on the ground. The store owner must have seen, because she yelled out through the doorway, "Mind you, and don't step on that egg. The old hen don't keer where she drops them."

Chapter 31

A crowd strangely reminiscent of yesterday was already packing the grounds around the church by the time we arrived. I saw a huge, hooded something that looked suspiciously like a black steel coffin. Several men were putting more wood on the flames under this monster.

Luke caught me looking and said, "Wait till you see what's inside." They raised the monster lid and there was a huge pig split down the middle. One of its eyes was looking at me.

"My lord, why would you leave the head on that thing to cook it?" I gasped.

"The brains and snout meat are some of the best parts," Luke said with a grin. Um, could I have some road-kill stew instead? The things they call food around here were amazing to me. Luke told me that when the porker was almost ready, hams and baskets of yams would be added to the mix. But I really wasn't paying attention to him, my mind being occupied by thoughts of how I would get to Atlanta the next day. I looked away from the pig and saw a hearse pull up on the side of the church.

Well, hell, at least it was a car of sorts. Maybe

the undertaker could give me a lift. If not he probably knew everyone in the area. Maybe he could give me some much-needed help.

I reintroduced myself to him, reminding him of the fine job he did at the wedding yesterday (like I heard any of it with all the goings-on that had been going on!) and told him my dilemma.

He listened quietly, just stood there like he was in meditation. I added that I would be happy to pay for the ride. Still not a peep. That gland was working over time. Calm and quiet he remained standing very erect in front of me and looking straight ahead not at all in my direction. His silence was getting on my nerves. In fact, I think I only had one good nerve left, and it was shredding by the minute. While yesterday he passed as a preacher, today he looked exactly how you'd picture an undertaker: very tall and bone thin, with a long neck, sharp, pointed nose, and deep-set eyes. He was wearing a black suit, a white shirt with round collar, and a black string tie.

Just as I was getting ready to get a choke hold on his bony neck for some response or sound to get some kind of answer out of him, he finally broke the silence. "I reckon I can take you," he said in a voice so low and slow it was almost a whisper. "I'm going to Atlanta to pick up supplies. Will be leaving early, about seven. You have someone drop you here at the church, and we'll go from there."

Could I ever be so lucky? "I will be here at

seven," I said, and thanked him. Who knows, or
cares, what supplies he was picking up. I'd be on my
way to New Jersey before he filled the hearse with
whatever gruesome tools of the trade he was going
to pick up at the airport.

"Be on time. I have to prepare for a funeral at
three," he admonished, then faded into the crowd.

I calculated the church was only three miles
from my air-cooled motel. Maybe Margaret or
Skipper could give me a ride to the church the next
morning. Oh hell, I would walk it if I had to. My
day suddenly had gotten a whole lot brighter. Even
the haze in the air was starting to look beautiful to
me.

I caught up with Sophie and Ralph and told
them about my arrangement with the undertaker.
Ralph started to laugh so hard he almost choked. I
said, "What's so damn funny?"

He said, "Make sure you sit close to the door,
and keep your hand on the handle. He may have
been a minister before turning undertaker, but nothing's sacred to that old boy. He's been married three
times and has ten kids. When he buries the hus-
bands, Luke said he goes courting the widows."

"Ralph, you gossiping old fool. Stop that talk
right now!" Sophie chided.

But nothing Ralph said could have spoiled my
mood. Now that I knew I'd be getting home the next
day, I started to enjoy being where I was. I wan-

dered over to the horseshoe pit, where a couple of fellows showed me how to pitch horseshoes. I then joined in the bag race, where we all pulled burlap bags up to our waists and attempted to run. I came in last place, seeing as I ended up almost having to crawl across the finish line. Pass the apple from one shoulder to another? I failed that one, too. But I was having a grand old time, sweating like hell but could have cared less.

Some women were sewing under the shade of a big oak tree. They showed me how they made the dollies, and illustrated their crochet and embroidery techniques. They tried to have me do a few stitches, but I just wasn't cut out for needlework. Instead, I admired a beautiful patchwork quilt three of the women were working on.

The preacher, who apparently hadn't been moonlighting at our motel last night because he showed up for church today, announced that the pig was done and the slicing, was beginning.

"Get your plates and line up for some good eating," he called. That was one call everyone answered, and I soon knew why. I never had pork tasting that good in my life. Add to it the slaw, cornbread, and baked beans, and I was in heaven. It was tough, but I managed to save room for seconds on the pork. This was a gain-five-pounds weekend, no doubt about that. I figured what the hell. I'd lose it soon enough when I was back home eating my own cooking.

I heard some folks talking about a fish fry come Friday night. I had to ask, "What kind of fish?"

One fellow said, "Catfish, of course. You ain't had nothing till you've eaten fried catfish with slaw and hush puppies. You'll never leave." Feline fish and quiet dogs? What kind of food is that, I wondered to myself. I decided it was best to leave that one alone. Besides, it was time for dessert.

Pecan pies, sweet potato pies, and my favorite, peach cobbler. No need to worry about leftovers, because there wouldn't be any. I was sure there were more people in that churchyard than lived in the next three counties. It almost seemed like a big family get-together, where everyone's happy and hungry. More families kept coming. Must have been the aroma of good food spreading throughout the dusty countryside.

I finally found myself in dire need of a rest room. I wiped the last of the cobbler off my lips with a paper napkin and turned to ask the woman standing next to me where that might be. She pointed to the back of the church. "Go around that side. It's closer."

I went around the side and looked back near the rear of the building. All I saw were two small white buildings with half moon-shaped holes on the door.

I thought; please don't tell me these are what I think they are. Like at that gas station on the way down, where you sit on a hole in a board and let gravity take over. "Go ahead," she said. "They are clean."

"Which one is for girls?" I asked her.

"Doesn't matter none. Just take your pick. Most folks go for the one that's empty. Here, I'll go with you," she added. Even when you're talking out-houses, we women just never seem to be able to go to a rest room unaccompanied.

I stepped inside, than quickly stepped back out again. "I hate to impose once again on your hospitality," I told her, "But there's no latch inside. How does one handle this situation?"

"That's what the red stick on the string is for," she said. "You put that through the hole, and then everyone can see that someone is inside."

"What an ingenious idea," I said. "Whoever thought of anything so clever?"

"Probably the first one who got themselves walked in on," she said, laughing. "Now before you leave, pull the stick inside," she instructed before leaving to get her self another piece of pie.

I pulled the door shut, stuck the string out the door and went ahead to do what needed to be done. Before I could finish, I heard the voices coming from the next shed over. There was definitely more than one person in there, and from the sounds they were making, they were giving the frame hut more action than it was designed to handle. I got out quickly, you can bet on that. Without looking to see who came out of the outhouse, I hurried back to the front of the church. There was still a half of pig left, which was a good thing; latecomers were catching up on some heavy eating. Lord have mercy if we would eat like this every day we would all have an ass the size of New Hampshire

Luke went over to his truck and came back carrying a guitar by its neck. He called out to Racer, the black fellow who had been in charge of cooking the pig, "Get your fiddle and let's have a Hee Haw here."

Racer went to his truck. He seemed to be moving even slower than the heat would dictate, and he seemed almost gingerly in his steps.

Luke said to Ralph, "Racer's never been too fast a man—that's how he got tagged with the name Racer—but he got even slower a couple weeks ago. That man's hurting real bad. He was doing the preacher's gardening, bending over to pull some weeds. Now the preacher has one of those Dobermans, a big, mean son of a bitch that he keeps for protection. That dog has teeth like a shark. That bad ass dog got out thru the screen door raced across the preachers property. Racer was bending over pulling weeds, his back was to the house. He never saw the Dobie coming until the dog took a bite out of Racer's ass.

"They said at the emergency room you could put a ball where that Dobie took his piece. The guys around here kid Racer that if the Dobie had centered more to the middle with him bent over like that, they would be calling him Rachel."

Racer painstakingly made his way over to us, his violin tucked under his arm. Someone offered him a chair; but he said he thought it best to stand.

I made my way through the crowd of folks sitting at picnic tables or on blankets spread out under the trees with their plates piled high with the wonderful food that I had too much of myself. I found a small bench near a shade tree. I sat down gratefully. By this time tomorrow, I'd be home, I thought. I could picture myself in my air-conditioned house, soaking in a mass of bubbles in my very own tub.

A voice broke into my daydream. "Are you with the family from up North that came for the wedding?"

Sitting down next to me was a rather attractive woman who was probably in her early forties. She had strong features and a friendly smile. She extended a hand that had shown evidence of hard work. I returned her warm shake.

"Yes, I am a close friend of the bride. Have you ever been up North?" She gave me a look that all but said, "been there, done that".

"Yes, I have been up North. I have a sister who moved up there when she got married to a fellow from Maryland. I guess my sister likes it all right living there, she never complained. By the way, my name's Melba Martin."

"Megan Riley," I said. "So tell me, Melba, did you like visiting there?"

"I guess it's all right if you want to live that way. I like the open space, though. People are more polite and friendly here. It seems to me, living up there nobody seems to have time for one another. The houses are all bunched together, then there's all that traffic. It's really too clustered everywhere you go for my liking. I went there another time for Christmas. There was a snowstorm. No one could get out for days. I never went back after that.

"Now enough about me," she said. "Are you having a nice visit here? What do you think about the South? Do you think you would like to come back?"

"It's my first visit here, and I'm only here for such a short time. I would have to have the time see a lot more of it before I could answer that honestly. The people here are friendly, but then I have been partying ever since we arrived. I am a city girl at heart, but I don't think that means I couldn't enjoy a vacation in quiet country."

"We folks here in this area are farmers. We have small houses on a nice piece of land. That's what keeps us fed and clothed, selling what we raise. When we have get-togethers like this, we forget the hard work and have fun."

"Do you and your family ever go somewhere away from here, like take a vacation? Aside from when you visited your sister, I mean."

"What fer," she said, laughing. "You get in a car, waste up all that gas to drive for a day, maybe two.

"You get a room that has a bed and a dresser but still costs too much just for sleeping in. Then you walk around not knowing where you are going, and you don't know anyone to talk with. Then you get some picture postcards, not knowing what to write on them. Folks buy those picture cards so people know you were there. Ha, you can tell them to save their money. Then the restaurant food ain't no way near as good as home cooking, and it costs more than it's worth. Then you're suppose to give the waitress money for bringing it to your table."

"You drive back home, the first thing you say is how good it is being home. Does that make sense? Why leave to begin with? Most folks take vacations to brag on where they were. Who cares? It's like they need to mix with strangers. Makes no sense to me, none at all," she said, shaking her head.

"We are given what is needed. There are things that everyone wants, but what you need comes first. Don't think we folks are poor; that's nonsense. We are fine. Always set a good table, and when the chill comes in, we have plenty of firewood around. We have fine friends who help one another. We work hard, but we work together as a family.

"Here I am just going on and on," she said. "What must you be thinking, me not letting you get a word in edge ways. By the way, you want a Co-Cola? There's some in that their steel tub, should be some cold by now." She called out to a man standing near the tub, "Lester, put a block of ice in with them drinks, would you?" She turned back to me. "It sure is hot today. But then again, it's been hot for the last six months."

"Say, honey, if you ever want to come down to visit here again, you are more than welcome to stay with us. I'll give you our address; you can drop me a line. I can't promise you an exciting time, but you've already been here, so you know about that. But I'll teach you how to make cobbler and some of the other Southern dishes. Take you out in the fields and show you how we grow peaches, pecans, and give you time to share with the family your life in New Jersey.

"Melba, I will certainly give your invitation some serious thought, and I thank you kindly for inviting me." We sat in silence for a few minutes, enjoying the day. I looked over at those giant kettles steaming on the food tables, and thought to myself, now if I had one of those, maybe I could make food half as good as what I had the pleasure of eating today. "Say, Melba, if you could have anything you wanted, what would you choose?"

"I'd get me one of those electric mixers I saw in a woman's magazine one time, with a couple of attachments, plus bowls. I mix everything with a hand beater. You know my biscuits and cakes. It's getting harder now that I'm getting older. Funny I should say that; my momma is almost eighty years old and she still mixes everything by hand. She wouldn't want one of them electric machines, can't trust them, she'd say. But as for me, I caught my hand in the washer ringer a couple of years back and it bothers me some when I am mixing things. Doesn't want to perform like it should. Who knows, maybe it's better to keep using it. Still, if I ever had some spare money I would like to have one."

She looked up and smiled as a tall, pleasant-looking man came toward us. Melba introduced him as her husband. He had come to collect her, he said. They had two milking cows that needed attention, and he thought it would be best if they left soon. We exchanged addresses. As she walked away, she turned and said, "Don't forget the invite. Would like to have you accept."

I enjoyed the shade for a few more moments after she left, but it felt a little lonely without her. I got up and went over to where Ralph was entertaining a couple of ladies with his stories. God only knows how many were true. "Where is Sophie?" I said, interrupting him.

"The last time I saw her she was headed for the privy," he said. "When Sophie gets back, we best leave," he continued. "Our chauffeur, the great pickup driver, Luke, said he has a hot date tonight, and he wants to get home and pretty himself."

That sounded fine; I would like that myself. Shower, wash my hair, and whip out my paperback book and read for a bit before settling in for the night. I was going to have a big day tomorrow.

Chapter 32

As soon as I got back to my room, I fell on the bed, and that's the last thing I remember until Sophie came knocking on my door at six in the morning. They were going to breakfast, she said. "Get dressed and have something with us before you meet Harper at the church."

I stretched, then got up and brushed my teeth. It didn't take me long to dress, and my bags were already packed, so I headed to the kitchen in no time flat with Missy at my heels.

I could smell the wonderful breakfast aromas even before I pushed open the kitchen door. Sophie and Ralph were already seated at the table, and Margaret was at the stove. Junior and Lume were nowhere in sight, which was fine by me. They'd be a little hard to take before I had my morning coffee.

I joined the table crew, and we chatted over breakfast about what a fun-filled time we had. Funny how soon we forget. But I didn't linger long; I was eager to get started, and I didn't want to miss my ride. I pushed back my chair when Skipper came into the room.

"Ready to go?" he asked.

"More than ready," I replied. I gave Margaret

and Missy a hug good-bye, then Ralph and Sophie.

"Don't forget to call me as soon as you get home," I told them.

"Don't you mean, if we get home?" Ralph said with a wink.

"I have no doubt you two will find your way back to New Jersey, even if it means stopping at every gas station and country store in between," I said, giving them one last hug before leaving with Skipper.

Thankfully, the ride to the church parking lot was uneventful. Mr. Haley was pulling the hearse in beside the steps as we pulled up. Skipper handed me my bags, then said a quick good-bye and turned the car back down the road toward the motel.

Mr. Haley said he had to get something from the church, and trotted up the steps and opened the door.

"The church isn't kept locked?" I said.

He stopped in the doorway, took his black hat off and wiped his brow. "We always keep it open for folks in need," he said. "Many times, when we have bad storms a person driving down the road can pull in and stay here till it passes. Sometimes folks just stop by to pray by theirselves. In hard times you have fellows walking the roads looking for work, and this church gives them a place to sleep come nightfall." He ducked inside, reappearing in moments.

My suitcase and garment bag were quickly transferred to the back of the hearse. I got into the front seat and said, "It certainly is a beautiful morning."

He looked straight ahead, grumbled something, and off we went. Maybe it was the call of the road, or maybe he had taken a sip of the communion wine when he stepped inside the church. All I know is, once we hit the open road, that man didn't come up for air the rest of the trip. Up until then, my experience with him was that he was the quiet type. What had gotten into him to turn him into Mr. Loquacious? I finally figured it out: After driving around with nothing but corpses for company, the man was overjoyed to be riding with someone who could listen.

We had to stop for gas, and of course I offered to pay for it. He refused to accept my money. I slipped him the bills anyway, saying "Here, put it in the collection on Sunday." He accepted grudgingly. Then he brightened up and started in on yet another tale about the wild and wonderful world of undertaking. That ride was an undertaking of a different kind, let me tell you. It may have only been a couple of hours' drive to get to Atlanta, but it felt more like a month. Must have been those Southern miles.

Chapter 33

Needless to say, we drew a lot of attention as the hearse pulled into the airport loading dock. Mr. Haley came around and helped me out, then went around to open the rear door of the hearse to get my suitcase and garment bag. As he was unloading, an airport security guard came over to us.

"So, are you waiting for a new casket coming into the airport?" he asked. "If so, you can park here for a while."

"No sir. For a change, I'm dropping off a live body," he said. They both looked at me, and then burst into a hearty belly laugh. I personally failed to see the humor. I quickly thanked Mr. Haley, and then made my way into the terminal.

I walked to the center of the terminal and looked in each direction to find the right line to stand in to get my ticket. I spotted the sign, and got in line. Everything was going my way that morning, it seemed. There were only two passengers waiting ahead of me. I glanced around the terminal, and noticed a tall, very good-looking black man wearing an expensive, white tailored suit and low-cut shirt several gold chains resting on his exposed chest. He was getting a lot of attention from the crowd around him, and he looked like he was used to getting fussed over. I had the feeling that, if he weren't getting the recognition he thought he deserved, he'd know what to do to make it happen.

He flounced across the center terminal, looking for all the audience like the main character in "Hello Dolly" coming down the red-carpeted ramp.

As he drew closer, I could hear his voice. He was doing a grand vocal imitation of Katherine Hepburn in one of my all-time favorite movies. I thought, "God, here comes the African Queen."

I made my way to the front of the line, and the agent had my ticket in order.

"Y'all are lucky to get on that flight," she said. "They were booked solid except for the two seats left in first class."

"You're right, I am lucky," I said. "For a change, things are going my way today." I paid the fare and asked what gate I should go to catch the plane. She told me, and said it looked like I had an hour or so to kill before my flight.

It was nearly noon, and I was hungry. I also needed something to drink after an hour and a half with Harper Haley.

The bar and lounge were jammed with people. On second thought, forget a sandwich. I figured it would probably take more time than I had to spare.

I ordered a Virgin Mary and settled onto a chair by the window. I heard that Hepburn voice, and turned to see the African Queen come floating into the lounge with his entourage.

"God, what a crowd," he drawled. "Who do you have to goose to get a drink around here?"

He ordered a very dry Bombay gin martini, telling the young waiter, "Don't bruise the gin. Stir it gently and add just a small lemon twist." I had never heard the word "twist" pronounced quite that way before.

As I sipped my drink, my stomach started talking to me. I mean, talking out loud. It didn't seem to remember the eggs, biscuits, and gravy I gave it earlier. I tried to tell it that it would get lunch on the plane, but the hunger pangs persisted. Somehow, the idea of airline fare, that four-by-six-inch plastic tray with various colored food-like items in it, just wasn't doing the trick. I was certain the inmates eat better at Leavenworth.

The lounge crowd also must have been concentrating more on drinking than eating, and the sound level was going up. The African Queen began to show off his new mambo step. Without music of course. As he minced and strutted, I overheard him bragging about how he learned to mambo while staying in Jamaica. Heaven help the person who got stuck sitting next to him on a plane, I thought.The PA system soon announced that my flight was boarding in five minutes. I finished my drink and headed to the gate. There were lines, long lines, and as usual people were becoming impatient. Why do they push and shove? I wondered. It's not like it'll get you a better seat, or get the plane to take off any sooner. I resisted the urge to shove back when a particularly belligerent fellow bumped me with his shoulder.

I finally made it through the door and was told to take a left to the first-class section. I could have the window or aisle seat because the other seat was also on a temporary standby. I took the aisle seat. Once we reached cruising altitude, there really wouldn't be much to see anyway.

I was comfortably seated with my seat belt secured, when I heard that voice. Oh no. There standing at my seat looking down at me was the African Queen. I hadn't gotten a really close look at him before then, and I felt the strangest feeling. It was almost like I knew him from somewhere, but I couldn't place him in the context of the airplane.

I must have waited a beat too long for his liking, because he began to get all huffy and out of sorts, waiting for me to get up so he could get past me to the window seat. I unhooked my belt, stood up and let him by. I started to sit down again, when he got up and said, "Dear me, this is never going to work. Excuse me again, but I must remove my jacket. It will be a wrinkled mess if I sit in this seat all crunched up to New Jersey."

Okay, gorgeous boy, I thought. Do what you

need to do. I waited, standing awkwardly in the narrow space while he fussed and smoothed and finally got his jacket folded in what he deemed to be the proper fashion. I thought we were done with this particular drama, until he leaned across me and tapped the passing stewardess on the arm.

"Do tell me the overhead compartments are kept clean," he said to her. "I would like to put my jacket there, but I can only if you can assure me it is spotless, dust-free, and scented."

Dear Lord. Where did he think he was, the Ritz? The stewardess, who should get the Miss Congeniality award should the airline ever offer one, finally got that squared away. We once again tried to get settled in our seats. I was struggling to get my seat belt rebuckled when the cabin door opened and a young man appeared.

"It'll be a few minutes before we take off. Is there anything we can do to make you more comfortable? If you need anything, feel free to ask."

My seatmate said, "Why thank you, just keep that thought for when we land." He looked the man up and down and said, "Are you the pilot?"

The young man in uniform said, "No, I am the radio dispatcher."

"That's okay, love. Everyone has to start somewhere." With the unbelievable grace of airline personnel who are trained to deal with just about everything, he managed a forced smile and moved

on down the aisle. Shortly after that, we were air-
borne. If I could endure the flight, I'd be home by
nightfall.

The stewardess came by and asked if we wanted
a drink. I ordered a much-needed Bloody Mary. My
seatmate ordered a Bombay gin martini. Between
sips of his beverage, he adjusted his chains and
looked at his three-inch, gold bracelet watch. He
glanced over at me.

"That outfit is not right for you at all."

"I beg your pardon?"

"Were you at a funeral?"

"No, I was at a wedding in Macon."

"Well, that outfit looks like a shroud. But how
appropriate. I did see you get out of a hearse."

I felt like Missy when someone approached my
door unannounced. The hairs on the nape of my
neck began to rise. I was ready for battle

"No, darling," he said. "It's really just all wrong.
You need bright, living colors, soft pinks, blues, a
lot of beige, not that slate-gray grim looking frocking dress."

"First of all, I did not wear this gray frocking
dress to the wedding," I said, steaming. "Secondly,
coming to the airport in a hearse is a long story I
don't need to share with anyone, particularly not
someone who is insulting my choice of clothing."

Just then the stewardess came by and asked if
we wanted another drink. He smiled and said, "Yes,
you may freshen my beverage.

"Here is my card," he said, turning back to me. "I am a fashion designer. I have a shop in the Village, that's in New York, you know. Come see me and I'll show you what you should be wearing. Being Hawaiian, I have the background to design clothing that'll not just make you look like a Polynesian queen, but make you feel like one, too."

Then it hit me like a bolt of lightning. That's where I had seen him before. It was that funky shop Sam and I had gone to after we had lunch with her mother. Sam told me he was from Hawaii. But could that suave shopkeeper really be the same man as the one sitting next to me? I looked closely at his face when he wasn't looking. Definitely the same man. I decided I wasn't going to inform him that I had already been in his shop, and in fact had even bought a pair of his sandals. I looked at the card he handed me. It said his name was Corbin. At the shop, he called himself "Corb."

Smells of something vaguely like a cross between dog food and overcooked broccoli wafted out of the galley area, and soon the stewardess came down the aisle pushing a cart with our "lunch." Corbin delicately sniffed at his, and nibbled a little at the edges of his salad and roll. He picked up a piece of his filet mignon, and then put it down with a little snort of disgust. "This steer must have died of rickets," he said. "And these three green golf balls, am I supposed to believe they are brussels sprouts? And this baked potato looks like it's had more air time than Lindbergh."

I was so hungry I actually ate all the filet of sole with lemon sauce, buttered noodles, and asparagus. I even ate the cake, which looked suspiciously like what they used to give us in elementary school cafeteria, might have been the same batch—it sure was stale enough. I think the fact that he was not enjoying his lunch made me enjoy mine even more. I sipped the chardonnay I had ordered to go with my lunch.

"I have pictures in my briefcase of my designs that were presented at the show in Atlanta," Corbin announced, poking at his steak. "I was down there for three days showing off my dresses." As he was talking, I slipped the card from my pocket. Corbin Duvall, Act II Fashions I discretely slipped it back into my purse.

"So you were down for a wedding," he said. "I take it from the absence of a ring on your left hand that you are either single or divorced."

I put down my wine glass, "What are we doing here, bonding? I wish you would put any interest you may have in my love life, sexual needs, and marital affairs to rest. You are beginning to irritate me."

"Now, now, let's not get testy. My question only required a simple yes or no."

"I don't care to discuss such personal matters with a complete stranger," I said. "With any luck I will never see you again. Now can we just have a quiet lunch?"

Obviously, that was not on the menu. "Know what they say about girls that never marry?" he asked.

"You don't know when to quit. It just may come as a surprise to your male ego, in which regard your cup appeareth to runneth over, but I've heard that sorry old line way too many times. It goes something like, 'If you're not a nun, then you are either an old maid, a lesbian, or a hooker.'"

"My God, you really are white, aren't you?" he said. "Believe me; none of those labels would ever apply to you. I know this fellow who enjoyed being a nun in drag. You wouldn't believe what went on under his frock."

"You know, I like being female. I have no problem being white. If you don't like it, that's your problem," I said. "At least I'm not afraid to be who I am. Can't say the same for you, trying to pass yourself off as Hawaiian. You're black, and you seem to be in very close touch with your feminine side. Nothing wrong with that, but it doesn't give you the right to go around slamming other people for what they were born with. How does it feel living a lie, anyway? How do your parents feel about what you turned out to be?"

"My mother died when I was just a kid," he said soberly. "I had to grow up without her being there in my life. But I still tell my mother everything that's in my heart. She knows and she understands."

"Is your father living?"

"Don't know if that son-of-a-bitch is living but if he isn't, I hope he knows what hell is about."

The man was all over the place, snotty then almost sweet. I couldn't make heads nor tails of him. Fortunately, the stewardess came by just then with two petite bottles of champagne and two plastic stem glasses. Corbin took a glass gratefully and tossed it back.

"God, this tastes like tiger piss," he said. I noticed that he finished the glass anyway.

He pulled his briefcase out from under the seat and showed me his designs. I hated to admit that they were very good, but they were. I was starting to like, and even respect, this man, despite the fact that he irritated the hell out of me.

We finally landed and taxied up to the terminal. Exhaustion was starting to fog my mind, and all I could think of were a hot bath and bed. We all stood up and waited for the signal to get off the plane. I felt a tap on my shoulder, and looked up to see Corbin. "See you in the Big Apple," he said with a smile. maybe, maybe not. Right now, all I wanted to see was the inside of my very own house. Even though I never did get around to finishing painting.

Chapter 34

As we all trooped down toward the baggage area, I tried to keep a safe distance behind Corbin. Just let him get his baggage and get out of my life. I was too tired to deal with his histrionics at that moment. Friends and relatives swarmed the passengers as we entered the terminal. Knowing no one was coming to greet me, I trudged off toward the luggage pickup area, with Corbin just ahead of me. Then all hell broke loose.

All of a sudden, time seemed to slow down. I was watching Corbin's well-shod back. A black fellow ran toward Corb, a shiny silver object in his hand. His other hand began to pull the gold chains away from Corb's chest. Another black man came up from behind and pulled the briefcase from Corb's hand. Then I saw Corbin going down, still in slow motion. The two black fellows ran out the terminal doors. I heard a woman scream, and realized from the harshness in my throat that it was me who was screaming. I saw Corb bent over holding his side. His body turned, and he looked straight at me as he fell to the terminal floor.

What had just happened? I kneeled down and lifted Corbin's head against my arm. I felt something trickling onto my skirt. Damn, it was blood, lots of blood. I could see it leaking from his left side and pooling on the floor. I screamed for someone, anyone, to get an ambulance.

I could hear a crowd of people gathering around us. I looked up and saw a ring of blank faces.

"Is there a doctor or nurse in the terminal?" I yelled. There was no change on those blank faces. Come on, people, we needed some help. I shouted again, "Did someone call an ambulance?" A man in an airport uniform pushed his way toward us. "There is an ambulance on the way."

"Oh, thank God," I said to him, then felt Corbin shift in my arms. "Corb, don't you go and die on me. Don't for one minute think I'm going to let you die lying here on the floor in the Newark Airport. You want to talk about class? How tacky can you get? That would be worse than pulling up to the Atlanta terminal in a hearse." I thought I heard some soft noise coming from his lips.

"Come on, Corb, help is on the way. And just think of what you're doing to your jacket." I thought I saw a ghost of a smile come to his face. At least he was staying conscious.

"Remember you said I would get fifty percent off of anything I liked in your store? Well, you better stick around to make good on that promise. After all, you're going to owe me a new wardrobe after bleeding all over this gray, ugly shroud, as you called it." I could almost feel him slipping away again.

"Hold on. Please, Corb, I hear the siren. Help is coming. Dear God, hurry." Two men in white rushed in with a stretcher. They heaved Corb onto it and started rolling him quickly toward the exit.

"Where are you taking him?"

"St. Elizabeth Hospital, ma'am. And we better hurry." They turned and whisked him off to the waiting ambulance, whose red flashing lights lit up the windows next to the exit doors.

I slumped against the wall. What happened? Why? Two men approached me and flipped open their wallets to reveal detective badges. One of the men, Detective Mikas, had his blond hair in a crew cut. He was handsome in a rugged way, and had a quiet manner. He appeared to be around thirty-five. Even in this extreme circumstance, I noticed that he did not wear a wedding ring.

His partner, Detective Ciccone, was shorter than Detective Mikas, and probably was about ten years older. He was almost bald, and his wedding ring showed signs of wear. He made no attempt at being friendly or pleasant. He just smoked one cigarette after another, and kept one hand in his pocket jingling his change.

Detective Mikas helped me to my feet, and then led me over to one of the airport offices. I sat down and looked at my bloody skirt, then started to cry.

He gave me some water and waited a few minutes until I could compose myself.

"Was the victim a friend of yours?" Detective Mikas asked. He seemed to be the designated interragator.

"No, we met on the plane. We were just traveling from Atlanta to Newark."

"Did he give you his name or where he lived?" I pulled out the card from my pocket and handed it to him.

"Can you tell us what happened?" I told them what I saw. I couldn't tell them exactly what the silver shiny object I had seen was. It could have been a knife or a gun, but I just didn't know. Detective Mikas told me it must have been a knife, because Corbin was stabbed, not shot. "Could you describe what the two men looked like?" he asked, popping a stick of gum into his mouth.

"No, they came running toward him, like from either side. Their backs were to me."

"Can you remember if they took anything from the victim?"

I thought for a second, trying to sort it all out. "I saw the one on the right take his briefcase. The one on the left had the shiny silver object, the knife, I guess, in his right hand. I saw his left hand go in front of Corbin—that's the name he gave me on the plane. When I got to him I saw that the gold chains he wore around his neck were gone."

"How many gold chains was he wearing?"

"I think two or three. I am not certain. Look, I am very upset. Can't we do this another time?"

"Sorry, ma'am, we have to ask these questions while it's clear in your mind. We won't bother you too much longer but we will have to have you come to headquarters in a couple of days to sign a statement, just a few more questions. Now were these two fellows black or white?"

"They were both black. They wore jeans, sneakers, and shirts with no sleeves."

"Do you mean like tank tops?"

"No, they were more like sweatshirts without sleeves." I thought some more, trying to think of any detail that might help them. "As I recall now, Corb was also wearing a wide, gold-band wristwatch. I cannot remember if that was still on his left wrist when they took him off to the ambulance or not."

"That's all right. We'll check that when we get to the hospital."

"What about Corb's luggage?"

"We have someone picking that up. It will be taken to police headquarters, and he'll get it back once we are through with the investigation. It's just a matter of checking the contents to see if we can't come up with a possible lead as to why he was stabbed coming through the airport." Detective Mikas ran his hand reflexively through his hair, riffling the crew cut. His partner sighed, like he was bored, and lit another cigarette. The air was becoming blue with the smoke.

"There are several aspects of this stabbing that will need to be thoroughly investigated," detective Mikas said. "We will need your name, address, and phone number, just in case we need to get in touch with you. Here is my card," he said, reaching into his wallet. "Should you think of anything at all, even if it doesn't seem like it could be important, please call me."

I scrabbled around in my purse until I finally found a pen and a scrap of paper. I wrote down my information and handed it to him, but it didn't seem to be enough. There must be something else I could do for Corbin.

"Will you call his store and let someone know what happened?" I asked. "Tell them what hospital they have taken him to. I don't know who else to ask you to call. I don't even know if he has any family, much less where they could be reached, but I'm sure someone from the store can tell you more."

"Yeah, we will do that when we leave here," detective, Ciccone spoke for the first time, glancing at his partner.

I noticed my hands were twisting the edge of my skirt, and dropped them into my lap. "I need to get my luggage," I said. "I cannot walk around with this blood on me; I have to get something to change into."

"Give me your ticket," said detective Mikas. "We will have a porter bring it to you. We will be in touch in the next few days. But please call us if you think of anything that might help us with this case."

He took off with my ticket, and within minutes a porter came into the office with my bags. Does one tip in these situations, I wondered. I must have been pretty dazed. I thanked him profusely, thanked the detectives, and probably would have thanked the clock on the wall if it would have gotten me out of that room.

I took my suitcase and garment bag to the ladies' room and pulled out a pair of jeans and a top. I took off the bloody, two-piece gray suit, rolled it up and put it into the case. I washed my hands and face, looked in the mirror and thought, you look like hell. As I walked through the terminal, I was wondering if I could make a cab materialize if I just thought about it really hard. A police officer walked up beside me, and tapped my arm.

"Are you the lady who was involved with the stabbing here?" he asked. I nodded. "detective Mikas asked me to drive you home. Let me take your suitcase. The car is just outside the door."

I just stood there and thought: When I left here just five days before, I was in a perfectly respectable car. This morning, I went to the airport in a hearse, and now I am going home in a police car.

"Are you all right, miss?" he asked, opening the back door of the car.

"Well as can be expected, I guess," I said, and off we went.

I was never so glad to see any thing as I was to see my own little house. The headlights reflected off my front steps, which seemed to be beckoning me inside. The officer helped me out, then handed me the suitcase and bag.

I unlocked my door and went inside, intent on a bath and a big glass of wine. I soaked until my skin got pruney, but decided to hold off on the chardonnay for a minute. I picked up the phone and called the hospital.

"I'd like to know the condition of a patient who was brought in tonight. His name is Corbin Duvall," I said. They were not about to give me any information, though, other than the fact that yes, he was a patient there. I sighed and hung up the phone. At least it sounded like he was still alive. He must have been, if he was a patient there, right? My mind was spinning, and I felt like I hadn't slept in twenty years.

Oh, Sam, I thought. I have been having one hell of a time since I left home to go to your wedding. Despite my exhaustion and worry over Corbin, part of me couldn't wait until Sam got back from her honeymoon so I could tell her the story.

The phone rang, and for a second I thought it

must be Sam, but it was detective Mikas. They had just brought Corbin from surgery, and he was stable. He told me that the surgeon felt he would make it just fine, even though he had lost a lot of blood. They repaired the deep stab wound, and he had an excellent chance of recovery.

I thanked the detective, then thanked God.

Chapter 35

Work was torture the next day. Everyone was asking how my trip was, but there was just too much to tell. I couldn't wait to get out of there. When the clock hit five, I bolted like a racehorse out of the starting gate, and went straight from the office parking lot to the hospital to check on Corbin.

I walked into the reception area, not certain what room number to ask for. Perhaps he was still in the ICU? The floor nurse behind the desk, a very young girl who looked like she was probably still in training, looked at his chart.

"Are you family?" Hmm, I didn't think I would pass as "Hawaiian," so I had to say no.

"I'm a close friend," I lied.

"Sorry," she said. "His card indicates family members only."

"But I need to see him. You see, I was with him at the airport when he was assaulted."

"Sorry, we have strict orders for family members only."

I felt someone move up behind me, and then a voice said, "It's all right. We'll take her with us."

"Oh, that's all right then, officers," she said. I

glanced over my shoulder and saw the two detectives from the airport.

Walking down the hall to Corbin's room, detective Mikas asked me again if I remembered anything more that would be helpful. I had wracked my brain all day, but I still couldn't think of anything to add to what I had already told them. We pushed open the door to Corbin's room.

Corbin was sitting up in bed; surrounded by so many flowers I felt I should have come to see him in a hearse. He looked pleased, though, and smiled when he saw me. Then he looked past me to the detectives, who were lingering in the doorway.

"We won't stay long," detective Mikas assured him. "But we do need to know if you can describe the two attackers. Did you recognize them from anywhere? Do you have any idea who they were?" Corbin just shook his head.

"Well, when you're feeling better, we would like you to come to the police station and look at some pictures. We'll bring your luggage to the hospital before you're discharged." The detectives left, and Corbin and I just looked at each other for a minute.

Strange that we had, through an accident of fate, become friends of some sort. What sort, I'm sure I couldn't tell you.

"Why would they keep your luggage?" I asked, trying to think of something to say to this near stranger I was now inexplicably connected to.

"Because they went through my things," he said. "Maybe they thought I was carrying some of the white stuff, or perhaps a gun. I'm sure they checked to see if I had a previous record—which I assure you I do not. That would give those bastards that attacked me more reason to get rid of me. I suppose they know by now about my personal lifestyle. Believe me; I'm sure they did a lot of checking. They probably know everything there is to know about me. You can't keep secrets from the police that's for sure. Other than my ethnicity and my flair, I am clean on all accounts, which I'm sure they were very disappointed to discover."

I asked him if there were anything I could get for him, but all he really wanted was to go home. I could relate to that, having spent altogether too much time in Macon wishing for just the same thing. The two of us could have been Dorothy without the magic slippers for all the good our wishing did us. But I finally made it back to my house, and the doctor said that Corbin ought to be able to go home by the weekend.

Corbin mentioned that the girl who worked in his store lived close by. She had already said that she wouldn't mind changing his dressings and checking in on him. He also had a close friend across the hall from his apartment who could go shopping for him, which meant he would not be totally alone. There was only one arrangement he didn't yet have covered, he said, and that was getting back to his apartment when he was released.

"How about I take you home?" I said. "Call me Friday and let me know if it looks like they're going to spring you on Saturday."

"You know, you're all right for a white girl."

"Cool it, Corbin. Don't push your luck."

Just then the nurse came in with a basket of flowers and another nurse with a vase filled with a dozen red roses. I said, "This room is starting to look like a viewing," and left. I stopped by the nursing station on my way out to leave my phone number.

Driving home, I let my thoughts wander to Sam and Harry on their honeymoon. I hoped they were drifting high on their cloud nine of marital bliss. Or at least that Harry had managed not to get bitten by an alligator down there in Florida. I cranked down the window to feel the cool breeze on my face and to dissipate the medicinal hospital smell that clung to me like smoke from one of detective Ciccone's cigarettes. I could not wait to get home and change. I had barely had time to peel off my work clothes and climb into shorts and a T-shirt when the phone rang.

"We are home," Sophie almost sang into my ear. "Ralph and I just got in. Ralph is all tired and grumpy as hell from unpacking the car, so I won't put him on the phone. I can't imagine what he's complaining about. I only bought a few things on the way home."

I laughed, then I heard a bark over the phone. "Sophie, that sounds like a dog in the background."

"Nothing wrong with your hearing, girl. You're right. We want you to come over Friday night for a cookout. Just hamburgers and salad stuff, say around seven? Then you can meet the new addition to our family."

"Sophie, where on earth did you pick up a dog between Macon and New Jersey?"

"Actually, you know her. It's Missy from the motel. Margaret and Skipper asked us if we wanted to take her. They were too busy to give her attention, and Ralph thought it would be company for me, seeing as I'm home alone every day. She was so good in the car. We just love her."

I'll bet she was good in the car. She was probably so stuffed full of sandwiches, pork rinds, and God knows what else, she must have slept the whole way.

"I can't wait to see her," I said. "We became pretty good friends over the weekend. Speaking of good friends, I don't suppose you've heard anything from our Sam since the wedding?"

"Well, no we haven't. How could we since we've been on the road since you left? Still, with her no news is good news. She would have let us know somehow if anything horrible had happened, so I guess we can assume that she is still alive and still married. I did speak to her mother earlier, but she said they didn't expect to hear from her any time soon. Said she'd call them when she was good and ready. She sounded really bitchy, but that's nothing unusual. Have you heard anything from her? How was your trip back?"

"Now that's a long story that I will tell you later. But I am fine, and that's all you really need to know. And no, I haven't heard a peep from the lovebirds either. I'm looking forward to seeing you all and Missy. What a story I have to tell both you guys!"

Chapter 36

Friday finally rolled around. I was heading home from work on the Garden State Parkway. What a drivers' nightmare. Everyone was headed to the beach for the weekend, and traffic was backing up all over the place. I spent the time wondering if Corbin would get out of the hospital tomorrow. Only two more exits to go before I could get off that bumper-to-bumper strip. I figured I'd call the hospital when I got home to see what the story was.

But I didn't have to. The phone was already ringing as I walked through the door.

"Get your chariot gassed and polished and pick me up at one tomorrow in the front of the hospital."

"Oh hi, Corbin. So nice to hear from you. Yes, I'm fine, thanks for asking," I said sarcastically.

I could practically hear him wave my comments away with the flutter of a hand. "And please be on time. I can't wait to get home. Oh, one thing more. Would you please bring a cold Coke? This house of medical detention thinks only one drink exists: ginger ale."

"Sounds like you're better," I said. "You are fast becoming a pain in the rear again. But I'll see you tomorrow anyway." I hung up the phone, changed out of my work clothes and headed over to Sophie and Ralph's house.

As I pulled up in front, I could hear Missy barking. I had stopped at the pet store during lunch to get her a toy, and I couldn't wait to give it to her. I parked the car and, dog-toy bag in hand, strolled up the walkway to the front door, almost bumping into Ralph on his way out. He grunted a greeting to me and kept on going.

"Why do you look so grumpy?" I called after him. "I am the one who had to sit in traffic." He turned around and came back up the steps to where I was standing.

"That Sophie really knows how to get me pissed," he said. "She has invited half the neighbors to this shindig. Now I have to go for more rolls, hot dogs, what else. Look at this damn list she had ready when I came home," he said, waving it in front of my face. "When I called her this morning, she said she didn't need anything. But that's Sophie for you. See you later," he said, and headed off to his car before I could say a word.

Missy came to the door and nosed it open. She gave me a great big lick, than began sniffing at the bag. She must have decided it was something good, because she grabbed it out of my hand and began shaking it. To her surprise, a rubber ham bone flew out. She jumped back, then crept up on it and poked at it with a paw. She then snatched it up with her mouth and carried it proudly into the house.

"That you, Megan?" I heard Sophie say. "Come out back. I am setting the tables. Want to help?" I wandered into the backyard and saw Sophie at work setting up chairs, stirring food, and generally acting busier than a hooker at a convention.

"I just saw Ralph," I said to her, picking up silverware to set the table. "He seems upset."

"He'll get over it. Always does. It's just that I, at the last minute, remembered it's Grace's birthday. You know Grace, lives across the street?" Without waiting for my nod, she continued. "I invited her plus her kids and the two grandchildren who are visiting. My friend Alice from up the street is coming, too—remind me not to let her wander into the living room." She laughed and gave the potato salad another stir. "And Luther's coming such a nice man. He lives alone."

"Oh, is he a widower?" I asked.

"No, his wife is dead."

I just shook my head and continued to lay down knives, forks, and spoons. Missy came racing out of the house and began throwing her new toy in the air, looking for attention. I went into the house to get some condiments, then came back out and set them on the table.

"Sophie, your kitchen already looks like a deli. Why would you feel you had to send Ralph out for more food?"

"You can never have enough food, you know. What's left, we'll finish over the weekend. Where is that Ralph anyway?" she said. "I think he's taking his time just to be spiteful. He needs to get that charcoal started."

I volunteered to get the grill going. I put on his apron, and fired up the coals. The guests started to arrive, so I put some hamburgers and hot dogs on the grill. Still no Ralph. Grace from across the street came over and introduced herself. She told me her husband just loved picnics; however, he worked from three to eleven as a chef. That accounted for his absence. I handed off the flipper to a man from down the block and went into the kitchen to see if Sophie needed any help there.

I was just walking in the door when Ralph finally arrived, carrying three bags and wearing a shit-eating grin.

"Well, it seems shopping agrees with you," I said.

Sophie entered the kitchen and saw Ralph standing there.

"So, you finally decided to show up? What the hell took you so long?"

"Sophie, you know that redhead that just moved in up the street?" he said, putting the bags down on the counter. "The poor dear was just coming home loaded with packages, and I stopped to offer her some help. She saw how warm and parched I was and offered me a cold beer. She has a ten-year-old daughter, and is getting a divorce. Lovely woman, so friendly," Ralph said.

"Who gives a shit," Sophie said and gave him a shove in the direction of the back yard. "Go take over the grill. I'll deal with you later."

Ralph laughed and winked to me. "Now I got her dander up. She's all kinds of fun when she gets riled." He went through the screen door singing "Love is a Many- Splendored Thing."

I had a couple of hot dogs and chatted with the neighbors, but it was clear that I wouldn't get the chance to tell Sophie and Ralph about my latest round of adventures that night. Plus it was getting late, and I would likely have a big day tomorrow. I made the exit farewell rounds, and then headed inside.

After racing around with her new toy and begging food for a couple of hours, it seems that Missy decided a nap on the sofa was about due. She was snoozing away, but jumped right up when I came into the room to give her a pat good-bye.

Sophie and Missy walked me to the door.

"Great barbecue, Sophie. I had a wonderful time," I said. "But—and I hope you won't take this the wrong way—it just isn't the same without Sam here."

"No, Megan, you're right. Everything was much too calm. A barbecue without Sam is like eggs without pepper. Still no word from her?"

"No, I haven't had a call yet. I'll let you know if she calls. You do the same, okay?" She agreed.

Just then Ralph came to the door and put an arm around my shoulders. "What's with you not saying good-bye to me?"

"Oh, I figured you were much too busy helping out all the lovely divorcees on the block," I said. On that note, I decided it was time to go.

"See you all later," I said. "I've got to get going on my way. Tomorrow promises to be a big day." "What do you have going on tomorrow?" Sophie asked.

"Oh, it's all part of a very long story that I would love to tell you about later. And I will, I promise. But right now I have to get to bed." I gave them both a hug, patted Missy, and headed off for home.

Chapter 37

I set the alarm for seven, thinking that maybe I could cut the grass before I had to leave to pick up Corbin. Or, I could always borrow a couple of goats from the adjoining farm and tie them out in strategic places on the lawn. I looked fondly over at the clock, remembering when Sam had given it to me.

We were both pretty broke that year. Sam needed some new furniture for her apartment, and I needed a new fridge, so we agreed we would skip our long-standing tradition of exchanging Christmas presents. Even though I was the one who suggested it, I found the perfect present for her and couldn't resist getting it. It was just three days before Christmas and I was doing some last-minute shopping. Passing the art store, I saw a painting of a poodle that looked exactly like Tyrone, her adored, pampered poodle and attractor of love interests, in the window. It almost looked like Tyrone had posed for this painting. I knew I had to get that picture, the devil with what we agreed to.

The painting was a bit pricey, but it would be worth it just to see the look on her face when I gave it to her, I thought. Needless to say, she was devastated when she opened the gift; joyful tears welled up in her eyes.

Sam hugged the painting to her chest and said, "Oh, Megan, this looks exactly like my dear baby Tyrone. It's wonderful! I only wish the gift I got for you was as fine." She looked at the presents she had lying under the tree, and grabbed one at random from the top of the pile with the casual flare she was gifted with.

"I was going to surprise you with this when we went out to dinner this week, but you might as well take this now. Go ahead, open it. I know it is something you will like, and of course it's something you need."

Now I knew this was a gift for someone else, or maybe it was something she had received. It didn't matter, though. I opened the box, and there was the radio/alarm clock.

"Yes, Sam, this is something I needed," I said, laughing. "And I'm glad you got me this instead of that fridge."

I smiled at the memory, turned out the light, and went to sleep thinking of Sam.

The morning dawned bright and, of course, hot. I managed to get the lawn mowed and get cleaned up before it was time to pick up Corbin. Driving to the hospital, I thought of Sam and Harry, and how much hotter it probably was in Florida than it was here in the cool North.

As I pulled up to the front doors of the hospital, Corbin was already there waiting in a wheelchair with his suitcase waiting beside him. He had a huge grin brimming with beautiful white teeth, and it got even bigger when he saw me pull up. The man was putting on a great performance for the two nurses who waited with him. He was being smiley and pleasant to them, so much so that I almost thought he got a personality transplant along with the stitches.

I rolled down the window, and called to him, "Hey, want a lift?"

"Oh heavens, yes. Thank you so much for coming to pick me up," he said and the nurses rolled him over to the car and helped him inside. He thanked them profusely, than waved at them as we pulled away from the curb. As soon as they were out of earshot, he turned to me and said, "Have you ever seen two uglier old broads than those two?" There's the Corbin I knew. I handed him over the soda he had requested. He popped the top and took a deep swallow.

"This Coke tastes like ambrosia," he sighed. "I am so happy to get the hell out of the hospital. They would not let me shower. They made me piss in a funnel. They kept waking me up to give me a sleeping pill. I had female nurses. The coffee tasted like dishwater. The only highlight of the day was when the doctor pulled down the sheet to examine me. God, he was a hunk. Sweet Jesus, it's good he made me roll on my stomach."

I rolled my eyes at him. He mimicked me, rolling his eyes back, until I had to laugh. He took another swallow, and then turned serious. "You know, lying there in the hospital, I really got to thinking about my life, and what's really important to me.

"I grew up in Georgia, did I tell you that?" he said. "In a small shack on a dirt farm in Georgia. We were poor, but hell, I didn't know that then. I was one of ten, not the oldest or the youngest, just sorta in between, you know. I was going nowhere, but then again, there was nowhere to go. We were never hungry, but don't remember ever being full, either. Guess none of us do. But my Momma did all she could to fill us up with love.

"She had this straw hat with flowers on it that she wore to church. One day I took the plastic flowers from her hat and put a real daisy in the brim. I went and gave it to her, feeling so proud of myself. She started to cry. I said, 'Momma, someday I will make money and buy you a new hat, shoes, and a dress. I'll buy you a bunch of flowers in all different colors, like we see at the funerals.' It was hard to tell if she was laughing or crying at that point.

"My dad was a sharecropper. We worked other people's land for a place to live and for food. My older brothers would make a couple of dollars going to the town, cleaning out stores, loading supplies. They worked all day and came home with a dollar apiece and handed it to Momma. Sometimes they would get a live chicken or maybe some flour or grain instead of a dollar. She would say how proud she was of them. We younger ones helped in the fields. Momma was out there in the fields all day until the day she died.

"One day when I was old enough, my brothers took me to town. I guess I must have been around twelve. When I saw the white women in their fine dresses and hats, holding parasols, I just stood on the street and stared. My brothers got mad as hell with me because I could not take my eyes away from what these women were wearing. How nice my Momma would look wearing a dress like that with a fine hat and a parasol. I finally stopped staring at them and went into a store. There were shelves of canned food, barrels of peanuts, and crackers—more food than I had ever seen in one place. Then I saw trays with wrapped candy, oranges, and apples. The man behind the counter saw me looking, and said, 'Do you want to work today?'

"I said, 'Yes, sir.'

"'Here is an order,' he said. 'Follow this lady and put these bags in her buggy.'

"She gave me a penny. I had never seen money before. I put it in my pocket, and then she handed me a peach. I saved that to bring home for my Momma. I worked real good, flashed my smile, and soon became a regular helper at the store. Whenever I had free time, which wasn't often, I would walk to the rear of the store where they had big rolls of dress material, laces, and heavy materials for curtains. I would just run my hand over them and think how fine they felt. Momma would look so nice in a dress made from one of these rolls, I thought.

"Unless there were sharecroppers like us in town that would give us a ride, we had to walk home from our town jobs. My brothers and I got home real late one Saturday and I was really hungry from walking home after working all day. But my Momma was not waiting on the porch like always. We went inside. There were a lot of women there and my Dad was crying. I started crying and ran into my parents' room. Two women tried to hold me back, but I broke loose. There was my Momma, just lying there so still. Her eyes were closed and she would not answer me. I said, 'Momma, why don't you open your eyes?' I felt my Dad's big hands on my shoulders. 'Your Momma went to heaven,' he said. That wasn't enough, but that's all he said. He took me outside and we all sat on the steps in silence. Then they came and took her away.

"Life went on, we got older. Dad got quiet. Then he got mean. Seems like when Momma died the good part in him died right along with her. He started beating us for the slightest infraction of his rules, and then he started beating us for no reason at all that I could see. Eventually he remarried, but that didn't seem to help. I didn't know how the others felt and I didn't much care. All I cared about was that my dreams of growing up and getting my Momma that fine dress and hat would never happen. Now all I could dream of was to get away.

"Then one day my aunt from New York came to visit us. Why, hell, I didn't even know that Momma had a sister. She didn't come to the funeral. It was hard to believe they were related, because that woman was nasty-looking, nothing like my Momma. She must have felt guilty about leaving us alone with the man my father had turned into, because she offered to take me and my brother, Clifford, back to New York with her. She had never married, but she had two boys of her own. Those two were bad seeds, let me tell you. I tried to stay away from them, because I knew they were heading for trouble.

"We lived with her and helped out in the small dress shop she had in the Bronx. I started to draw pictures of dresses that I would have wanted my Momma to wear. I drew them whenever I wasn't cleaning the shop or waiting on ladies. Let me tell you, I could sell dresses better than my aunt could. Charmed the hell out of those fat black, women, too. One day a salesman who came to the shop fairly regularly saw my pictures. He asked my aunt who drew them, and she told him I did. That was how I got started.

"This salesman got me a job in the garment district, the center of the world of fashion. I started cutting there, but kept working on my designs. I saved every cent I could. Then I saw a shop for sale, a dinky little storefront in the village. I painted it mad colors, hung curtains, and put two sewing machines in the back. I got a couple of people to come in and work in the sewing shop at night. I bought cheap bolts of materials, leftovers mostly, and made dresses. Every dress was made thinking of my Momma.

"I didn't waste a thing, either. I used the leftovers to make scarves that could be thrown over the shoulder of the dresses. At first, I could only get three mannequins in my small front window, but business started coming in, eventually getting really good. I moved to a larger place and got more seamstresses. One time, I met a designer from an uptown shop who said he wanted me to work for him. I said, 'I worked for someone since I was ten years old, and that was enough of that for me.'"

He sighed. "When I was in Atlanta, I went to my Momma's grave with fresh flowers. Weeds had taken over, but I found her. I took a dozen red roses and one daisy. I also had a long talk with her. She knows where I am and who I am. I also told her what I am, because I was always truthful with

Momma. I could tell that she still loves me. As I stood there at her grave, I felt her arms take me in close to her. She told me, 'Who you are, Corbin, why that's fine.'

"That's about the best thing a child could ever hear from his Momma," I said, feeling a little teary myself. "She must have been a very special woman."

"You know when this whole thing happened at the airport," Corbin said, "I swear I saw my Momma standing there, just smiling and holding her arms out to me like she did when I was a kid and hurt myself. I wanted to run into her arms, but for some reason I could not reach her. Someday I will be able to, though. And I know that she'll accept me for everything I am."

"But Corbin," I said, "How would she feel about you pretending to be of another race altogether?"

"She'd understand, at least I think she would. Yes, I pass myself off as a Hawaiian, but what choice do I have? She'd know the kinds of problems I'd face. I mean, how far could a young black guy make it toward having his own shop in New York, coming from a dirt farm in Georgia? Or Harlem for that matter. Maybe someday it won't matter, but it sure does now."

"But how the hell did you come to decide you were Hawaiian?" I asked. He started to laugh.

"You know, I was in a store looking at travel brochures and I picked one up for Hawaii. It looked like a nice place to be from, and everyone had a tan, so why not?"

"Not to sound ungrateful for your baring your soul here, but why are you telling me all this?" I asked.

"I am telling you all this shit because you saved my life. Now you are responsible for my Hawaiian black butt."

We both burst out laughing, and were still giggling when we pulled up in front of his apartment. A young man and his sister were waiting for him on the steps. Before he opened the door I turned and kissed him on the cheek.

"How about I call you when you are feeling better? I would like to see your shop."

He said, "How about you and I having dinner some night? Maybe a luau?" We shared a smile.

"That's fine with me," I said. "I'll bring the leis."

Chapter 38

Driving away from Corbin's place and heading back to my own, I thought how great it was that now everyone who was connected with the wedding trip to Georgia was home safe and sound. Even Missy now had someone to share her life with. I pulled into my driveway and climbed the steps to my porch. I riffled through the mail, and made myself an iced tea. Life was good.

Still, the people I met and experiences I had down there left me wanting more. Down the road at the age of ninety, I could envision myself sitting in a wheelchair on the wraparound porch of a Prickly Pines Home for wayward geriatrics who don't know where they were or why they were there, but didn't give a damn either way. I would suck my puréed dinner up through a straw and think back on those five days I had getting to and from Macon, and all the rest in between. I took another sip from my iced tea and pretended it was a mint julep.

But what if my make-believe nursing home went coed and I ended up having Corbin Duvall, a.k.a. the African Queen, occupying the room next to mine? I could picture him sitting at a tabletop sewing machine, strobe lighting overhead, making designer short, and flannel nightgowns with matching jock straps for the males. Dear God, hear my prayer, I thought. When it's time for me to go, please let me go quickly.

Chapter 39

Life started to settle back into the usual routines, with a few exceptions. One was that I still hadn't heard from Sam. This was highly unusual; she had never gone this long before without calling me about some fool thing or other she'd gotten involved with. The other exception was the ongoing police investigation into Corbin's stabbing.

Despite my telling them that I only saw the assailants from the back, detectives Mikas and Ciccone came out to my house to pick me up and drove me to the station to look at books of faces. Seeing as I could only have recognized the backs of their heads, this did little good. When I called Corbin to tell him about it, he didn't seem to be surprised.

"What do you think of the detectives on the case?" he asked me.

"Detective Mikas seems competent, and kind of nice, too. But that detective Ciccone, well, I could do without seeing him again."

"Yeah. He must be a real thrill to live with," Corbin said. "His wife does nothing but cook pasta every night and have babies. His idea of a wild Saturday night out is a six-pack of beer and salami sandwiches in the yard."

"Corbin, how would you know that?"

"Bill Mikas told me. He came to the hospital a couple of times to visit. I mentioned to him what a hard case detective Ciccone was, like a mean macho. I know he knows what I am, and he acts like he thinks I deserve what happened to me. Bill said he went to his place for a cookout. The guy had hot dogs and the cheapest beer they brew."

I awoke the next morning, a Sunday, to the usual ritual on my street. It should be a quiet little cul de sac, with just twenty houses on it and a farm in back. The problem is that the houses are tightly grouped in the form of a horseshoe, which leaves little privacy from any angle.

The ritual goes like this: There are three men who work the night shift who usually get home about seven-thirty a.m. They immediately throw up the garage doors, whip out their lawn mowers, rev up their engines, and let the mowing contest begin. When their lawns look like the heads of new Army recruits, the three cut their engines, bang each other over the back, and whip out a six-pack to celebrate. Once the beer is consumed, they raise the hoods of their cars, stand there, and look inside, twist or turn a few of the plugs or wires, pull out the oil stick, and slam the hood. They finally disappear when their wives call them in to eat.

I lay in bed and listened to the motors revving, then twisted the button to turn on the clock radio to drown them out. I just wanted to lie there for a while. The weather would be hot and humid, the radio said. Possible thundershowers tomorrow. I thought of all I had to do that day. Get up, have coffee, run errands, and spend the afternoon at a pool. The one good thing about having Sam be incommunicado is that I finally had time for more of a social life with those of the male persuasion. Jeff from the office invited me out for dinner that night. He'd be picking me up around seven to try a new Japanese restaurant.

The merry mowers were buzzing away, the radio was going, but neither was enough to drown out the sound of the phone ringing. Who would be calling at eight on a Sunday morning?

"Hello?" I said, hoping it would be Sam. But it was Corbin, of course.

"I know this is short notice, darling, but I am having a few people in for a brunch around noon-ish. I insist you come."

"Corbin, my life has been on short notice for several weeks, but I really did have other plans." Like lounging around. "Is there some special occasion for the brunch, or some other reason I really have to be there, darling?"

"You really are bitchy early," he said. "The reason I want you to come is that I want you to meet my new friend. Actually, it has passed the friendship stage, but there is no need to get into that with you."

"If you'll be frank with me, I'll be frank right back at you," I said. "I'll have to say no, I can't make it. I have plans to soak some sun at the pool with friends."

"God, girl, you can still do that. Get a life. But do come. I am having a new rum punch. I picked up the recipe in Jamaica—the island, not Queens— plus marvelous hors d'oeuvres. I'll be expecting you," he said. "Ta ta."

So much for a quiet day. He had my curiosity on high. What could the African Queen possibly sur- prise me with after what I had been through with him already? The thought that got me out of bed: What would I wear?

Chapter 40

Driving to New York on Sunday at noon is an out-of-body experience. Half of New Jersey must spend the day in the tunnel. The traffic was bumper to bumper.

Before going to Corbin's, I stopped at the corner flower shop and bought an assorted bouquet; the selection was not that great considering the price.

I hadn't really registered it when I dropped him off the day before, but his building was a well-kept brownstone. I went through the door and saw several names listed, with black buttons beside each name. I pushed the second button and heard a buzzer go off at the door. There were no elevators to the second floor, so I climbed the stairs. Standing outside the door, I heard sounds of several people talking at once, music, and laughter. I knocked on the door, which was half-open, and walked in. I didn't see anyone I recognized; there was definitely no sign of Corbin. Someone came up from behind me, took the flowers and disappeared, saying "I'll go put these in some water." I did see a gal pouring rum into a large bowl filled with fruit.

I went over to her. "Could you tell me if I'm in Corbin's apartment?" I asked, feeling foolish.

"Yes, he will back in a few minutes. He just ran to the deli at the corner. Well, more like hobbled," she said. "But he insisted on going himself. At least he took his new friend with him to help.

"Would you like to test the new drink?" she asked as she stirred the rum and fruit with a glass ladle. "It's Corbin's new creation with coconut milk and high-octane Jamaican rum."

"I think I'll pass for now," I said. "Perhaps later." I walked to the large window facing the street, and saw Corbin coming around a corner with two store bags. Then I saw another man join him. No, this could not be possible, no way. The two men were looking at each other and laughing themselves almost silly. It was Corbin and detective Bill Mikas. Corbin beamed at me as he entered the room. "I knew you would come," he said, giving me a one-armed hug. He handed me a glass of a somewhat vile-looking liquid.

"Here, have some of my new Tasmanian Rum punch. You look like you could use it. This is Bill Mikas. I know you two have met," he nodded to me, then turned and smiled at the tall, broad-shouldered blond man. "We have become friends, and I wanted you to share that because you were part of how it came about."

More people were coming in the door. Corbin said, "Float around. I'll catch up with you later." He spun around and, with much of his old grace, went to greet the newcomers. Hard to imagine that just yesterday he was in the hospital. That Coke sure is a miracle medicine, I thought. Or maybe it was just being free of doctors and nurses.

I strolled around his apartment, which was very tastefully decorated. My heels sank into the deep, red-living room carpeting. The furniture was black and white, and he had some very good paintings on the walls. I stuck my head in the kitchen and saw that it was cheerful, with a lot of pots and pans hanging from large hooks from the ceiling. Everything was white—the cabinets, walls, and kitchen set with glass-topped table. My flowers were placed in a milk-white knobby vase in the center of the table.

Corbin and Bill were filling large platters with finger food. Bill left the room to deliver several of the filled plates to the hungry crowd. Corbin smiled. "Guess I blew your mind, right? Bill came here yesterday to check on my condition and to ask me more questions concerning the stabbing. Then he and I just started talking, and we haven't stopped since."

"I'm sure he was very concerned about your condition," I said dryly.

"No, it isn't like you may think—we are just friends who have something in common it's not like you show me yours, I show you mine. Anyway, I didn't ask you to come here just to tell you about my new friend. There is something else I must tell you about the incident at the airport."

Now he had my attention. "Corbin, why do I feel that I do not want to hear this?"

"Remember when the two came at me? I didn't get a look at them—I was too busy being stabbed— but I did see a third guy standing like off to one side just before I was attacked."

"Did you know him?" I asked.

Corbin nodded. "He was one of my aunt's boys. He is a couple years older than me, and he was always in trouble. My aunt never named his father because he was put in jail soon after my cousin was born. His father was stabbed in jail and died, she later told me.

"After I left my aunt and went out on my own, she told me my cousin had been arrested for assault and robbery, and when he got out of jail he moved to New Jersey. He and his brother hang with a rough crowd now."

"You told the police about him, right?"

"No, I didn't want to say anything because of my aunt, she was good to me. I mean, she did her best to get me away from my abusive old man. She is very ill and this would only hurt her more than she deserves."

"Corbin, are you crazy? That's withholding evidence," I said. "What if he knows you saw him? He knows who you are—for Christ Almighty's sake, he knows who I am! Suppose he decides you're going to tell me, which I wish the hell you hadn't. That makes me just as dangerous to him as you are. Where in the hell are your brains, Corbin? He could be watching us right now," I said, instinctively glancing around me. "What if he saw you and the good detective doing the old bed and breakfast routine? If you don't tell your good friend Bill the whole story, I will," I said, grabbing his face in my hands. "Here, read my lips. I will tell him."

"You don't understand, he could deny the whole thing. He could say he was just at the airport, that he never came toward me. I know he recognized me in the split second that I saw him, but he was just standing there. They cannot convict someone for just standing in the terminal."

"They can as accessory to the crime. You could have been killed!" I exclaimed, feeling like smacking some sense into him. "Just because you are alive right now, don't think there's some law saying you are going to stay that way. You should, in good conscience and to save your ass, have him picked up for questioning. He will have to tell the police the names of the two that attacked you. They may not necessarily convict him in your attack, but at least you could get those two put away and save someone else from being attacked." I grabbed his hand and gripped it tightly.

"Maybe next time they will kill someone; it could be you or me." I dropped his hand and sighed in exasperation. "I can't believe we are having this conversation. Don't you realize how serious this is? Or perhaps you just don't give a damn."

Bill came into the kitchen and handed me another glass of rum punch and a small plate of snacks. "You two look so serious," he said. "I hope this talk isn't about me."

I looked at Corbin. He smiled and pressed Bill's hand. "Of course it's about you. I'll tell you later."

"Megan, let's just drop this morbid conversation for now." I shot him a glance that could have done him more damage than the knife at the airport. "Yes, don't look at me that way. I will tell him, I promise. But for now, why don't we just go out and mingle with my guests?"

"If you don't mind, Corbin, I really have to leave. Don't forget to tell Bill what you promised me here in your kitchen." I made my way out to my car.

Corbin ran over as I was opening the door. "I am really pleased you came don't worry, I will straighten things out. That's a promise. I will call you later this week." He turned to go back inside, and then looked back at me over his shoulder.

"One more thing. That gal who was making the punch? She is a criminal lawyer, a real nice gal. She thought you were real nice, too. She would like to call you to meet for dinner sometime, or a drink. Whichever."

"Corbin, you tell Ms. law and order that I seriously plan on enrolling into the Morristown Convent tomorrow morning."

"Girl, you can't do that. They only take Catholics."

"I'll fake it," I said, and slammed the door.

By the time I reached my driveway, the heavens opened and poured out a monsoon of rain. Thunder roared across the area, and I could smell the ozone from the lightning striking nearby on the air. I finished up my chores around the house, had some supper, and prepared to spend a perfect evening soaking in clouds of bubbles, and finishing the book I started at that motel in Georgia.

The ringing phone was not part of the plan I had in mind. The idea was to ignore the sound and just get on with my book. Whoever was on the other end did not share that thought. It must have rung twenty times before I finally relented and picked it up.

"Hello? Is that you, Sam? Where are you? Are you and Harry home already?"

"No, silly I mean Megan. Guess what?" Uh oh. Sam's "guess whats" could be frightening experiences. I straightened my shoulders, stiffened my resolve and said, "What, Sam?" So she told me.

Chapter 41

After spending the night tossing, turning, and staring at the luminous green hands on the clock that weren't respectful enough to move to a faster beat, I was not exactly rested, refreshed, and ready for another Monday when the alarm went off. Sam's call from the night before had me twisted up in knots. Why did she even bother to go through with the wedding? No, I decided, slapping the button to shut off the alarm; the alarm clock that Sam had given me. Stop it, I told myself. Enough of that. I'd been wrestling with my thoughts on the latest situation she had gotten herself into—and the revelations she shared—all night long. It was time to get ready for work. I pushed myself out of bed and started my morning routine.

Coffee truly is a miracle drug. After two cups, I was ready to face the traffic I was sure to have to endure on the way to work. In the summer, I have to leave at least an hour early to get a head start on the masses of weekend beach and sun worshipers returning to work. I had to search all over the house to find my briefcase, which I usually leave by the front door before I finally remembered I had left it in the car.

I climbed into the car and snapped on the radio. The weatherman was predicting another hot and humid day. "For those who can get away, the weather in the Bahamas will be dry with balmy breezes," he said. Like who gives a shit? I thought, blowing a stray piece of hair off my already sticky face. I hoped I'd be able to look reasonably presentable for the eight o'clock staff meeting. The weekly booster meeting is the only time the CEO graces us lowly workers with his presence. Between his luncheons and golfing meetings—the purpose of which, of course, was to promote contracts and stroke the local politicians—he leaves us pretty much on our own. Thank the good Lord for that. If he didn't, the place would have closed years ago.

Pulling into my designated spot at the plant parking lot, I saw the gal that does the typing for several of the department supervisors. She had the small cubicle next to my office, and for some reason, she had designated herself as my assistant. She was standing at the top of the steps looking like she was going to burst if she couldn't tell me her news in the next few seconds.

As I walked up the steps to the door, she tried to whisper in my ear, but she was so excited that she almost blasted my eardrum.

"You had a call from a detective from the NPD."

"The what?"

"You know, the Newark Police Department.

detective Robbins. He left his phone number for you. You are supposed to call and ask for him, like ASAP."

Like, sure. Like, my Monday was really getting off to a good start. first Sam, now this.

I closed my office door and dropped the brief-case on my chair. My desk was already piled with stacks of files and correspondence that I needed to get to right away if I didn't want to end up spending Saturday in the office. I shoved some papers to the side, located the phone buried underneath, and thought I should have hired that short, chubby, slow-moving gal I interviewed last spring. Instead, I had to hire a dynamo who had the mail opened and sorted and was waiting for her next assignment before I even had time to get some coffee. I sighed and dialed the number she had given me.

"This is Megan Riley returning detective Robbins' call. Is he there?"

"Yes, this is he," the voice on the phone responded. "We need you to come to the police sta-tion."

"May I ask why?" I said, thinking my week was already shot to hell.

"There was a shooting early this morning," he said. "We have reason to believe it could be con-nected with the incident to which you were a wit-ness at the Newark airport."

Oh no. Corbin? "May I ask who was shot?"

"I'd rather not get into it over the phone," he said. "Please come down to the precinct and we can go over more of the facts in detail."

"But I already told the detectives at the airport all I knew. I really don't know what else I could add to my previous statement. Why can't you tell me who was shot?"

Well, that Newark version of Kojak wasn't going to budge, that was for sure. He proceeded to give me directions to NPD, and told me where I could meet him once I got there. "So, I'll see you in about fifteen minutes then?" he said, adding, "Be sure you park by one of the yellow signs in the front of the building. The other spaces are all restricted areas." He politely hung up the phone.

Why is it that police stations are almost always located in the least desirable, most unsafe area of a city? Maybe the powers that be think that having police stations that look bad will scare the criminals. I dutifully parked by one of the yellow signs, and was accosted by a derelict-looking, half-human being asking me for a buck. I was already so worked up; I almost jumped out of my skin. If any time of my life I was going to have cardiac arrest from severe fright, it would have happened right then.

A patrolman getting out of his squad car came from across the parking lot, spotted me, and came over to see if I needed any help. The derelict moved on, and I went into the police station.

It looked even worse than the last time I was there looking at mug shots. The inside of this station had all the decor of the black hole of Calcutta. heat, body odor, and food smells were circulated by two large fans positioned at each end of the room. All they accomplished was blowing the mixture back and forth like a huge, noxious bubble. There was a raised platform like a speaker's podium, flanked by two large trash cans that were overflowing with the refuse from the nightly menu: pizza boxes and fried chicken containers.

I wandered over to a wooden table that had a chair propped next to it. It was empty except for a phone, what looked like a half-eaten donut, and a styrofoam cup that was leaking murky-looking coffee down the side. I figured with time it would make it to the floor to blend in with other stains. And I thought my office was bad.

I stared down at the desk, my mind going blank. All I could think was that I just wanted to get out of there. Then I heard a voice coming from behind me. The jailhouse clerk said, "If you will have a seat, I'll have someone get detective Robbins for you. Would you like a soda or coffee?"

"I don't think so, thank you," I said, looking around and shuddering.

The outside door banged open, making me jump, and bounced off walls that looked like they'd been banged many times before. I could see dents and smears of metallic paint at the level of the doors' handles. Two women and I use that term loosely, were shoved through the door followed by a big man in uniform. Using the best of their foul, descriptive English, they screeched that they knew their rights; they wanted to call their lawyer.

The officer wasn't taking it from them. He said loud and clear, "Sit down, shut your mouths, and behave yourselves. You know what will happen if you're held here for a couple nights away from Daddy." They plopped themselves down on a bench, muttering to each other and shooting him nasty looks.

I heard a raspy voice then saw detective Robbins come over and pull up a chair next to me. Not a bad-looking fellow, I thought. He was a bit pudgy, but tall enough to carry it at about five-eleven. His suit looked like it had done some hard time through its years of service with him. No ring, I noticed, but I had a feeling he was more at ease interrogating someone with a rap sheet than sitting across a candlelit table from the opposite sex.

He said that all the rooms were presently being used, and he did not want to discuss the reasons I was called until we could have some privacy. He offered me a soda, then remembered that the machines were empty and wouldn't be refilled until the vendor came at ten. I planned on being long gone before then. He left with the promise that I would be called as soon as possible. All that kept running through my mind was that Corbin had been shot. The man may have driven me crazy, but I liked him. Please, God, let it not be him.

My thoughts were rudely interrupted by the women on the bench. One was black, the other looked Spanish. They both looked far older than their years.

"Lookee who we have visiting with us today," the black girl said loudly. "Grace Kelly has come to the Newark the House of Detention. They must be making a movie: 'The Night Life in Newark.'" She laughed raucously and nudged her friend. "We can be a big help to you, girl. Just ask us what happens in the dark here on the third shift. Know what I mean? What naughty thing did you do? Come home to Mommie without your panties?"

The younger one said, "Rose, leave her alone." Now Rose didn't seem to like that at all.

"Daisy, who do you think you're giving orders to? I am Big Daddy's main squeeze, so don't go messing with me, bitch. How would you like to go with me to the emergency room? 'Cause girl, we are going to need them doctors to get my foot out of your Mexican ass."

The door banged open again, and the girl who was shoved through appeared to be another member of their family.

"Violet, what're you doing here?" Daisy said. Violet joined them on the bench.

"I was doing this trick, and he refused to pay, can you believe it? So I just kinda hit him in the face with a piece of wood that was kinda laying there, and he kind of fell over as his pants were kinda down around his knees. I took his wallet and ran like hell out of the alley. Ran right in front of a patrolman."

Rose looked bored by the story and by her coworkers in general. She decided to start again with me. "Girl, what are you here for? Like what are they busting you for, sweetie? Did you run away from home?"

Against my better judgment, I replied, "I really don't know why the detective called my office to ask me to come here this morning."

Rose threw her head back so far that both her feet went up into the air. She let out a roaring laugh. "Well, girl, that's the first time I ever heard that one."

Then Rose, who had a set of teeth that looked like piano keys, said, "Damn, if that doesn't beat hell's drums. This prissy white girl is sitting in this shit hole and doesn't even know why. My Momma tells me how dumb I am; well, she should meet you. "Least I know why I'm here."

I asked Rose, the apparent group leader, how come they all had the name of a flower.

With much pride, she informed me that Big Daddy, their professional guidance counselor, named all his girls after flowers. "We are Daddy's 'flower girls,'" she said, sounding proud of herself.

Oh please. Come on, detective Robbins, I prayed. Just get me out of here. Thankfully, I finally heard the door open, and Detective Robbins motioned that I should follow him. We went into another, much smaller room. Seated at a table were three other people: a female lawyer searching through her briefcase, a black man in handcuffs, and Corbin. I was flooded with relief. Corbin was all right! He gave me a feeble wave.

Detective Robbins began speaking, directing his comments to the woman with the briefcase. "What we have here is a black male; age twenty-nine, with several known priors. He was in the store when the holdup was taking place. He was carrying a gun when he was caught running from the rear exit of the convenience store.

"We have a dead black male that was shot in the store by the owner, who was also armed. The deceased was wearing gold jewelry that was stolen from a Corbin Duvall during a stabbing and robbery at the Newark airport. He also has been identified as one of the robbers by a bystander."

He nodded at Corbin. "We have had Mr. Duvall here since early this morning to make the necessary identification of his gold watch and two gold chains. The deceased was a cousin of Mr. Duvall, who at one time lived with his aunt and her sons. She currently resides in Brooklyn.

"The deceased, together with his brother, have been stealing for a long time. They were picked up by the police several times for other juvenile crimes. Their mother is too ill to be present here today."

Detective Robbins looked at the man in hand-cuffs, who had been sitting sullenly throughout the recital. "Perhaps it is better she should not have to see her one son shot dead and the other arrested.

"Our prisoner here," he nodded at Corbin's cousin, "will hopefully be persuaded to tell us who the third person was at the Newark stabbing and robbery.

Detective Robbins then turned to me. "Do you recognize this man from the airport?"

I had to be honest: I truly did not. "I had only seen them very briefly from the back," I told him. "Everything happened so fast. I just didn't get a look at their faces."

Detective Robbins stood up and said, "Well folks, except for the paperwork and whatever future procedures will be necessary, we're done here." He looked at me and Corbin, "You two can leave for now."

In the hall Corbin broke down and began to cry. I put my hand on his arm and whispered; "Now you can get on with your life. That's what you have left, make the most of it."

He said, "When I identified my cousin at the morgue, he was wearing my jewelry. I feel so much sorrow for my aunt. No one deserves this." He looked at me, agony in his eyes. "How can I tell her what happened?"

"You will find a way."

The door opened, and detective Robbins came over to Corbin.

"We will notify you when we can release the body for burial. We will, however, have to keep your jewelry until after the trial."

Corbin, still sniffling a bit, nodded, and we left the station. The heat blasted us as soon as we set foot on the pavement outside, but it felt good after the stuffiness of the station.

I dropped Corbin off at the Newark terminal where he could get a bus back to the city. "I'll catch up with you later," I told him.

Chapter 42

When I first got summoned to the police station, I had thought I would be able to get back to work in no time. But I was going to have to take the rest of the day off. My concentration was shot. What I didn't need was to go back to work and try to catch up on the work piling up on my desk, then face the heavy traffic to get home.

Now that the episode with Corbin looked like it was being put to rest, I should have been able to just get on with my life, I thought as I drove home after stopping back at the office to make my apologies. But I couldn't. That telephone conversation I had with Sam when she called me from their motel in Florida the night before was haunting me. It was the first time we ever got mad enough at each other to actually get into a shouting match. I remembered several times when she was dating and I could not keep my opinion to myself. It usually got me in trouble, but we'd never had this kind of disagreement before.

So I went to Sam's wedding, and I saw how happy she was. I must admit I wasn't too happy to see her high-school heartthrob at the reception. The one thing she doesn't need is any encouragement toward promiscuity. I knew damn straight that Sophie and Ralph were just as displeased about him being there as I was. I wondered for a moment how he could have found out about the wedding, but then again, I guessed country news travels faster then the daily papers.

When Sam called from Florida, I knew something was again brewing in her mind. She wasn't coming back to New Jersey, she said. It seems at the wedding reception when her high school "love" and she were dancing, he told her he was just in Macon to visit his parents. He was now living in Florida. He had a successful car dealership and was doing very well. His mother had mentioned that Sam was here for her wedding, so he had thought he would drop in at the reception to see her, she said. He gave her his card and asked her to stop by when they get into Jacksonville.

The more she talked about this, the less I liked hearing what she wasn't saying.

She told me her high-school romance, with Harley Veneer, was long over with. "Harry and I did stop at his place in Florida," she said, "but it was just to take a break from driving."

I thought, Sam, surely you don't think for one minute I am buying this.

"What a place Harley has," she gushed. "He must have six people working for him, plus he has a really nice apartment above the showroom. He said he's building a service department next to the showroom.

"And guess what?" she continued. "He was telling Harry how he could use a top-notch mechanic. That he would pay twice what Harry made on his own. We went for lunch, and he was telling Harry to think about his offer and stop by on the way back with his answer. Harley told us how low the cost of living was there. And no snow and icy winters. They are building new tracts of houses just a few miles down the road dirt—cheap compared to up North. I could have a job as office manager at the dealership, which would free Harley up to, spend more time with the customers and train new salesmen."

I was thinking that this guy Harley could sell more than just cars; he could sell shit on a stick and she'd be buying it by the dozen.

"Harry and I are in a nice motel near Disney World; it is really great here," she continued. "Harry has had so many surprises for me. We took a walk last evening, and we went into one of those convenience stores. We bought a can of that whipped cream and box of fresh strawberries to have later. We didn't eat all of them—you would be surprised what else you can do with whipped cream and strawberries!"

"Where is Harry?" I asked, thinking he certainly would not want Sam discussing his bedroom playtimes with me.

"Harry went for a swim. He loves the pool. But Megan, we are talking a lot about the offer from Harley. I don't think we'll be coming back to New Jersey."

"What do you mean, 'we're talking', Sam? You mean you are doing most of the talking. I'm sure poor Harry doesn't even know what hit him."

That's when the conversation became loud and unfriendly.

"There you go again!" she exclaimed. "You make me sound like I'm always conniving. I just want what's best for Harry. I told him I hoped he was giving this offer serious thought, because I know a chance like this can only come once in our lifetime. I know he wants me to have nice things, and with this job, he could afford it. Plus he would not have to work in that old wooden garage he rents that gets so cold in the winters. We could afford to buy a house, instead of having to rent a tacky little apartment. I told him, "Why should we have to wait for years to get what we both could have now?""

"Sam, if I ever run for office I certainly would want you for my campaign manager," I retorted. That really pissed her off. The tone of her voice hit a double-octave pitch, which only happens when her defenses kick into overdrive. She was going to let me have it. I could picture her tugging on her ear and wishing it were my neck she had her hands around. I knew I was going to get both barrels. Sam did not let me down.

"Listen, girlfriend, love may be a many splendid thing but it doesn't pay the bills or buy the nice things we want in our lifetime. How many chances do you think we're going to get to live the good life? Yes, I care about Harry, but you know as well as I do that love is basically bullshit. Look what happened to you. Look what happened to me." I could hear her breathing hard, like she was running for her life.

"I decided a long time ago that love is bullshit, men are bullshit, and the whole thing is just a big steaming pile of shit. There isn't a man on earth I would feel emotionally safe or secure with."

"Sam, what's the matter with you?" I said. I had never heard her talk this way before.

"Oh, there isn't anything the matter with me. I'm just fine. I know how things work. After all, I learned everything I had to know about love and trust from my own dear parents when I was just a kid." She paused, and then began again in a softer tone, almost like she was thinking out loud.

"A girl's daddy is the first man to protect her from bad things, to love and cherish her, right?" she said. "A girl's daddy shouldn't expose her to things she's too young to understand, and then just go on like nothing happened. I was too young to understand then, but I understand it all now, and have for a long time."

"What are you trying to tell me, Sam?"

"See, my Daddy meant everything to me when I was little. He was the nice one, the one I could go to with my problems. He protected me from my firewater-breathing mother. She was drinking more than socially, and the best times I could remember were when she would have retired to her room with one of her 'spells' when I came home from school. It was much worse when she was up and lurching around the house, demanding, yelling...

"One never talked about it, of course. Southern ladies like my mother had a high standard of responsibility to maintain. She would never allow herself to be seen out socially without her husband, and she'd never go into a store to buy alcohol. She'd call a cab and send the driver to purchase what booze she wanted. And she wanted a lot.

"I used to lie awake at night waiting for Daddy to come home from another late night at the office, just praying that nothing bad had happened to him. I couldn't sleep until my father's car would pull into the driveway. He wouldn't raise the garage door and wake my mother, but I'd hear him. Only when I knew he was home safe could I sleep. Little did I know."

"Sam, are you sure you want to continue this conversation? You can stop right now and we will never speak of it again."

"You know, keeping all these dark family secrets

Chapter 43

to myself has always seemed safer than airing them out," she said. "But I think it's about time I told someone besides the three shrinks I spent years of sessions with since I left home. You can really piss me off and I am angry as hell with you right now this minute, but you listen to my wild stories, and you never criticize me unless you feel you have to because you're worried about me. I also know, I really do know, that you are my best friend ever."

I could hear a catch in her voice, then a deep sigh, as she continued. "You're the only real friend I've ever had," she said. "You're different than other people. Most people, once they get close to you they want to know everything about you, and I just can't have that. Men are the worst. They can do whatever the hell they want to whenever they want to, but when the bastards want to get married they look for the only virgin in town. Then starts the first degree: what are you doing with your life, questions about your family, how many guys you've dated. I told that son-of-a-bitch dentist that I had screwed all the dentists in town. He took off like a shot. Same with all the other guys I've dated. They thought after a couple months of dating that they had a right to know everything about me. But it's okay for them to act like my father and lie about their past.

"Daddy has been doing that his whole life, you know. Lying about his past. People always thought he was a handsome, sophisticated, well-bred example of what a father and husband should be. My friends at school thought I was so lucky to have such a great dad, and their mothers envied my mother. Well, I had some big news for them."

"What, Sam?" I coached. "What about your father?"

"Well, one weekend when I was ten, my mother took the car and spent the weekend with Memaw, who was feeling poorly. I went with her to the farm. Thankfully, Memaw wasn't seriously ill. I think it was just that she missed seeing her daughter and I. Mother was always a softer person when she was on the farm with her parents, and that was one of the few times I felt safe alone with her. We left very early Sunday morning because the weather forecast predicted heavy storms. Mother did not like storms, you know. She would sit in her room with the shutters closed when there was lightning outside.

"When we got to our house I saw a car in our driveway. I said, 'Look, Momma, we must have company.' The house was very quiet. Momma told me to go to my room and close the door. I did, and no sooner was the door shut than it was like a hurricane blew through our house.

"I heard my mother screaming, 'I thought you stopped this! You promised this would not happen anymore. And you, whatever your name is, get the hell out of my bed and my house. Take your clothing, put it on in your car, and anywhere, just get out of here. I don't care if someone sees you stark naked. Where is that gun? It won't matter where I shoot you. This is some horrible mess. You are both very sick and disgusting. Your daughter is just down the hall!'

"I heard the front door slam, and the car started and pulled away. I could not hear my father saying anything, just my mother screaming 'How could you? You never did stop, did you? Answer me, you son of a bitch! Tell me again how sorry you are. This never ended, did it?

"All this time you have been doing this. All I had to do was just come home early to find you and your low-life screwing in my bed."

"I could not, I mean not, think my mother knew the words she was using. She had gotten her second wind. 'Why did you marry me, have a baby with me? Was it just to cover up your sick, demented sex orgies? I just came from telling my parents how well we are doing; you certainly shot hell out of that glowing story! I came home and what do I find? A stark-naked man in my bed, with his arms wrapped around my naked husband.'

"That was when I finally figured out that the person she was calling queer, gay, sick, and homosexual was my father."

There was total silence on the line. I couldn't think of a thing to say to her.

"When I was seventeen, I started going out with Harley, though we'd known each other what seemed like forever. He wasn't like the other boys; he was the one guy I could marry, I told myself. That's what we promised each other when we were eleven. He gave me a ring from one of those cereal boxes. I still have it.

"Then one night when we were having dinner, Mother said, 'Samantha, your father has been offered a good job in Bayonne, New Jersey. We are moving up there, near where Uncle Ralph and Aunt Sophie live.' She told me he had already accepted the job, the house had been sold, and the moving truck would be there the following Saturday. She told me to pack the things I wanted to take with me.

"Well, that just blew my world straight to hell. I had to leave my friends, leave Harley. I loved him, and I loved that old house in spite of the haunting, terrible secrets hidden within those walls.

"It was so final, like everything for the past seventeen years of my life had been erased.

"And I knew the reason why, too. It wasn't for any job, let me tell you. As time went on, I was certain my father was still seeing that man. That's why mother wanted to get away from there. Her Southern pride would never allow any family or friends to know what my father was doing. Divorce was out of the question for her; she would stay married and take his secret to her grave. My parents still went to social functions together, family gatherings, church, dinners with friends. They performed their marital obligations in public so well that they would have fooled the Pope. In the privacy of our home it was a different story, though. They never spoke to each other unless it was something concerning maintaining the house or about me."

"Did you ever tell your mother or father that you knew his secret?" I asked.

"No. What purpose would that serve? It would only add more pain to dredge up something that was never going to go away, never change, never get better, never. My third shrink tried to convince me that it was my mother I was really more angry with for putting up with his sexual desire for men. I told her she's right, I hate the woman for not taking me and leaving. She put her own selfish reasons—what people would say or think—first, and made me grow up sharing her hell-on-earth life with a husband that would have preferred to share his life with a man. She said my father's love for me and my mother probably were sincere, and that someday he would be able to say to me, 'I'm sorry but I cannot help my preference.' Maybe he set himself up that weekend, hoping to get caught, hoping that once my mother saw the way things were, she would let him go. Maybe it was the only way he knew to tell her that he had no other way of being.

"I realized then that my mother could not tolerate loving a man who could not be her husband in a true sense. She was going to make him pay. The shrink said that she was sure Mother didn't realize that her decision to stay with her husband made me a victim of her deep bitterness and resentment.

"So that's how it is with them today. My father goes away on his so-called fishing and business trips with his male friends. That's totally acceptable. He's very discreet about spending weekends with his male lovers at their places in the city. He always comes home before the cock crows on Monday morning. Under her sweet Southern manners, Mother continues to seethe. And life goes on."

"But Sam, you have choices. You don't need to turn your marriage into a travesty like theirs," I cried. "Harry loves you. Please think about what you're doing, moving to Florida and working with your old love. You don't have to live your life in reaction to your parents' mistakes."

"I don't plan to make anyone make restitution for the mistakes my parents made," she said stiffly. "I am their only child, and I am the only one who has to bear the scars of their poor judgment." She sighed.

"I will go on trying to put as much of the past behind me that my heart will allow, but please do me a favor. Don't judge me for any decisions I make. Just remember my happiness at you being there for the most important day of my life. I will never forget how proud and pleased I was to see you standing there at the church when I got out of the car. I am not ever going to ask how you feel about everything I told you.

"Guess what?" she asked.

"I know, I love you too."

Chapter 44

Harry and Sam came back to Newark after their honeymoon in Florida. They brought their lab puppy, Blaze, who had traipsed all over Florida with the lovebirds. Sam had snuck him into the hotel rooms in her bag, she said.

They had a lot to settle before moving down to Florida. Harry sold his business to a buddy of his, and Sam gave notice at her job and got someone in the office to take over her apartment lease. I helped her pack the things she wanted to take with her back to Florida. Harry packed up his tools, and they had her furniture sent to Florida to be put into storage until they could buy a house.

Between all the packing and settling of affairs, I managed to tell her all about Corbin, and she was dying to meet him again. She remembered him from our shopping spree earlier in the summer, and couldn't wait to renew the acquaintance. Despite her feelings about her father's gayness, she just fell in love with Corbin when the three of us met for lunch in the Village near his shop. He remembered her from our shopping trip before the wedding, telling her that she was one of the best customers he had all summer. Once the dishes were cleared off the table, he pulled a box out from under his chair. "A late wedding present for you," he said. She opened it, and squealed with delight as she unfolded a fire-engine red muumuu.

"It's perfect! Oh Corbin, just imagine how I'll be turning heads down there in Jacksonville when I show them what a little New York style looks like." "Just be sure you don't go turning the wrong heads," I warned her, but she just shushed me and laughed. As we walked out the door of the restaurant, she pulled me aside and whispered, "I just love that man. Maybe I should introduce him to my father." Dear Lord, she was getting to have a sense of humor about her family situation. Maybe she's finally starting to heal. I could only hope, for her and Harry's sake, that it was true.

Ralph, Sophie, and I took them out for dinner the night before they were leaving. It was sad, but happy at the same time, if you know what I mean. They looked so excited about their new venture that I couldn't resist feeling that everything might just come out okay after all. I promised to visit them next summer. Harry also made it known to me that the decision to take on this venture was his, which helped to settle my mind a bit.

Sam and I went to the ladies' room together. After doing the essentials, we sat down on the counters by the sink to take a few minutes together. I asked how her parents were taking the news about the move.

"When Harry and I stopped by their house last Friday night, my father, of course, was not at home. Mother said he was working late," she rolled her eyes at me and sighed. "We only stayed about an hour. We told her our plans. She looks so much older these days. I guess with all of the excitement at the wedding I didn't notice it before.

"Harry went ahead of me when we were leaving to get the car started. Mother dearest put her hand on my arm, looked in my eyes, and said, 'Samantha, I hope y'all know what you're doing.' I could smell the bourbon on her breath. That really just pissed me off. I felt like I was going to blow up at her. My father would rather be with his boyfriend than say good-bye to his only daughter, my mother is an alcoholic who can't even manage her own life, much less provide a decent upbringing for her child. And she had the nerve to question my judgment! I managed to hold it in, though. All I said was, 'Well, Mother, if I am making a mistake at least I will be the only one who will have to pay for it.' I left her staring open-mouthed at me in the doorway.

"Daddy did at least call last night after we got home from dinner. He said that Mother had told him we were moving to Florida. 'I'm sorry I was not there when you and Harry stopped by,' he said to me. 'I hope you will keep in touch. You know how much you mean to us. Your Mother and I did the best we could for you, and we'll always be there for both of you if you ever get into a bind for money. I love you, Samantha, always remember that.'

"That's how my parents reacted to my leaving. I hope that answered your question; it certainly answered mine." She sighed, and then took my hand in hers. "At least I know I'll always have you, Megan. You know I will call you often."

"And I'll call you, too. And maybe I can come down on vacation and visit you next summer," I said. Like wild horses could keep me away. I wanted to keep a close eye on what that girl was up to, let me tell you.

The next morning, I went over to her house to say one final good-bye. Harry was putting the final boxes in the car, which was sagging under the weight of what looked like hundreds of boxes already stuffed into the backseat. Sam came out the doorway, took one final look at her former home, and then resolutely shut the door.

"Oh, Megan, I'm getting ready to start a whole new life," she said. Then she leaned over and kissed me on the cheek, then stepped back and looked me straight in the eye.

"Guess what?" she said.

"I know, Sam. Me too." I saw a tear drip down her face before she straightened her shoulders, patted her hair, and turned to start down the walk to where Harry was waiting by the car.

"Honey," she called to him, "like the shepherd said to his sheepdog, 'let's get the flock out of here.'"

I laughed through my tears as I waved good-bye. I watched the car until it disappeared around the corner.

That was just two weeks ago, but it seems so much longer than that. Everything has been so normal and quiet with her gone. I guess that's a good thing, but, as Sam would say, it also kind of sucks. At least I still have Corbin to liven things up a bit when I get the urge to be irritated into action.

So I sit here on my bed, ready to set the alarm for another day, when the phone rings.

Who would be calling me at eleven-thirty at night? I smiled to myself. Who else? I grabbed the phone.

"Hello?"

I heard a quick breath on the other end, then Sam's voice. "Guess what?"

—The End—

A Wedding In Georgia